Please return/renew this item by the last date shown

worcestershire
countycouncil
Cultural Services

TRIANGLE OF FEAR

A man is running away, but no one follows him. He runs to a hiding place he knew as a child, but it is crumbling, day by day. He finds there a man and a woman, pretending to be housekeepers. Who are they? Murderers, traitors, spies? Then suddenly he realises that they too are waiting to escape. From what? There is no one to be seen, yet slowly the shadow of death creeps in. They watch each other, wondering who must meet death first . . .

*Books by John Newton Chance
in the Linford Mystery Library:*

SCREAMING FOG
THE DEATH MATCH LADIES

JOHN NEWTON CHANCE

TRIANGLE OF FEAR

Complete and Unabridged

WORCESTERSHIRE COUNTY COUNCIL
CULTURAL SERVICES

LINFORD
Leicester

First published in Great Britain in 1962 by
Robert Hale Limited
London

First Linford Edition
published 1998
by arrangement with
Robert Hale Limited
London

British Library CIP Data

Chance, John Newton, *1911 – 1983*
    Triangle of fear.—Large print ed.—
Linford mystery library
    1. Detective and mystery stories
    2. Large type books
    I. Title
    823.9′14 [F]

    ISBN 0–7089–5397–2

Published by
F. A. Thorpe (Publishing) Ltd.
Anstey, Leicestershire

Set by Words & Graphics Ltd.
Anstey, Leicestershire
Printed and bound in Great Britain by
T. J. International Ltd., Padstow, Cornwall

This book is printed on acid-free paper

Atmospheric

He could not understand why the theatre had no stairs, why he had to squeeze through little openings in thick walls that, when he was trying to struggle through them, raised the panic of claustrophobia in him. Now he came to another landing, where one edge of it dropped sheer into the empty auditorium, a hundred feet below.

As he trod the concrete platform the edge of it began to crumble, and the air became rare with fear. Yet he had to go on, further upwards all the time; he dare not go back, for he knew that, as he got through the tiny openings, they closed behind him.

He came out on to the roof, and the slates were tattered and crumbling, and there were holes where the rafters showed through like rotting bones. Up the slope ran a rusty iron ladder, up which he must climb into the rare air of the sky.

1

As he gripped the ladder, the rust cracked away and a rung fell, ringing on the slates, then tumbled over the edge of the roof and spun away down into a great chasm, at the bottom of which little houses stood.

He watched it fall and the rotten ladder shivered under his own shivering of fear.

But there was no way down; he must go on up and up the steep ladder by the crumbling roof. The slope seemed to tilt as he went up, until he was climbing vertically, then almost as if it overhung him.

The ladder began to come away from its fixings, slowly, with little bursts of rust. Slates began to fall away from the slope and fall, spinning dizzily away into the vast depth of the chasm below him.

The ladder bent, iron crumbling under his weight, and then he began to fall, slowly, hanging breathless in the vast emptiness.

And suddenly he was in the house again, but it was huge and so big that he seemed to reach no higher than the door handles in the great, sunlit corridor. He began to run along the passage, but his feet were heavy, and he was slow with fear and the thumping pursuit of his own heart beating.

He saw the Spanish lady in the big room as he ran through the door, and she smiled at him, and he was big with the excitement of her, but he had to go on, for somewhere in the house was the room of the mysteries, the masks, the horrid waxen effigies and the musty terror of clothes that only the lifeless wore.

It was the place of the secrets, where Jim would be, and he must find Jim or be crushed when the pursuers came up behind him.

His footfalls echoed in the maze of great corridors and the ceilings seemed to grow taller and farther away from him and he felt the house was growing so big, and he so small, that he would never be able to search the place in time.

But then, echoing through the corridors he heard Jim's voice calling, and he stopped, bewildered by the number of directions from which the voice came.

'Gary! Gary! *Gary*!' It was slow, like a mocking laugh; yet colourless as a dead man's face.

'Jim!' he called, making a trumpet of his hands.

The vastness of the place swallowed up his voice.

'Jim! Where are you? *Jim*!'

He knew now that he was small again, and had a boy's fear of being found in a guilty place. He must find Jim and get out of the house before They came and caught them both.

He began to run along the corridors, opening the huge doors, pulling aside curtains, looking into cupboards. And then suddenly he ran into the room where there was no floor and he began to fall into blackness so that his heart stopped beating and breath came no more . . .

The sheets were wet with his sweat. He sat up and they froze on his body in the hot night.

'Jim,' he said, his voice harsh with dryness and fear. He put his hands to his wet face, then threw off the bedclothes

4

and got out of the bed.

Across the room the wide, uncurtained window stared down over the broad panorama of the city lights, like tramping glow worms in velvet. There was silence in the place save for a faint humming from a faulty bell transformer in the hall.

He crossed the bedroom to the luxurious bathroom, where the city lights glowed on the ceiling. He did not turn on any lights. It was as if he was scared of light, and would have hidden in the dark.

He stepped under the shower and turned it on himself. His pyjamas came like silk, clinging to his big, fine body. He stood feeling the relief of water on his skin, turning his open mouth up to the cooling spray.

He stepped out at last, pooling the floor until he took off the garments and threw them into the bath. He got a big towel and began to rub down, trying to feel normal.

'I can't go on,' he said aloud. 'My nerves are going. I've got to get out of it. Got to get out. Must go away

5

from it. If I stay it means breakdown, and after that — worse. There must be a way . . . '

He stopped moving altogether.

'Jim? Why Jim? After all these years. Twenty years it must be. Jim. When we used to break into the house . . . He went and we were going to write and then it faded away and he had gone. He has still gone. Why did I dream of him? I've often dreamed of the house, but he's never been there . . .

'But I didn't dream of him. I just called for him, and somebody called for me. It's my head. I can't clear it. My brains burn like smouldering wool. There's only fear and sickness of Something Coming. I can't go on.'

Now, suddenly, he switched on lights. He dressed quickly and went out of the flat, slamming the door behind him. He lit a cigarette going down in the lift, watching the little indicator lights flick on and out, impatient to get to the bottom.

He looked at his watch, but had forgotten to put it on.

He opened the lift doors and crossed the empty vestibule with its rich, fresh smell of the banked flowers there. The silence was absolute when he stopped by the swing doors for a moment, as if there had been someone following . . .

He went out and on the curve the Bentley stood gleaming with the richness of night, its long open body seeming endless as a great silent ship. He got in. The green-eyed clock winked three-thirty, and as he started and went quietly to the gates, the first grey light of dawn showed like a flush behind the edge of the great flat block.

He went out into the deserted roads and headed back through the years out of fear.

1

The Bentley went silently along the narrow, rutted lane. The dappled shapes of the beech trees ran along the bonnet, spilling off the shining paint in a stream of dazzling sun. On either side of the track, slender, trembling fingers of self-sown birch touched the sides of the fleeing car and stayed shivering after it had gone.

He stared ahead, his light grey jacket tossed on the seat beside him, a wallet slipping out more and more with each slight motion of the moving car. His white shirt was undone at the neck, his tie pulled loose. The ashtray on the dash rebelled with the crumpled ends of cigarettes.

He began to slow, as memory puzzled him. The place was so much smaller than he remembered, and the lane seemed to be growing narrower, closing in on him, choking.

Then between the slender trees of the wood he saw a sturdier mass of trees, and the sun was mirrored on the surface of a lake.

He slowed right down and then stopped. The track was high. To the left the ground sloped away, carpeted with red leaves of a past autumn, down into a dip amongst the little trees. For a moment he sat there, looking from the dip across to the mossy rocks overhanging the mirror of the lake. For a moment the sweet breath of escape became pungent with the sadness of nostalgia; the sweet, tormenting memory of a boyhood by this lake, twenty years ago. There had been no trouble then, no regrets, just the normal healthy fears of retribution that had been a firm, quick and understandable thing.

Now the troubles came like a ghost army behind him, shadowing his every thought, making him flee with their shadows though he did not know that they yet moved to catch him.

He restarted the engine, but it was still running and the starter hissed in protest. He moved the car forward, steered it to the left facing the dip amidst the self-sown birch and poised it on the edge. Then he got out, turned off the engine and let go the brake. The big car rolled slowly down into the dip, flicking the little trembling leaves aside, and when it came to rest in the hollow, the shivering screen of the little trees hid all but the sudden gleam of a bright part catching the sun shafting down between the arches of the trees.

He turned towards the lake and stood, staring at it, his hands in his pockets, feeling the cigarettes and matches, the loose change. He went up on to the top of the rock, where he had fished all those years ago, and he stared down into the smooth mirror of the lake, where some insect made ripples that laughed at him like a distorting mirror.

On the left side of the lake the thick trees stood in great ranks, and behind them, he remembered, was the big house, the place of the ghosts and the daring expeditions, of breaking into the empty lodge and drawing battle plans on the walls.

Again he heard his mother's voice across the years, telling him never to swim in the lake, because it had no bottom. But he had swum and felt a queer thrill at feeling nothing was below him, a pit perhaps that reached down into the middle of the world. The very feelings of his boyhood were stealing back, partners in the last escape.

He unfastened his tie and watched it dangling from his fingers, wondering whether to leave it there, on the rock as a pointer for when They came.

The voice came suddenly, with an effect so shocking that he remained still, as if he had been hit. He turned and saw the girl there, staring at him with no attempt to hide her antagonism.

She was tall, and her jeans showed long legs, like a dancer's. Her shirt, half open, not entirely hid her big, pointing breasts. Her hair was somehow scragged back from her perfect face, with a coil or a bun behind that he could not properly see. Her eyes were blue and flecked with the changing colours of the sunlit lake, and bright with a fierce suspicion. Her

12

mouth was rich as a split plum, but firm almost with the twist of hatred.

She had a double-barrelled gun which she held pointing to the ground by his feet.

'What are you doing here?' she repeated.

Into his tormented mind came the sudden idea that the girl shone with a queer kind of savagery that made her want to shoot him.

But tumbling over that came the cold rivers of despair, filling his soul with the knowledge that his escape was suddenly, completely destroyed.

The blazing challenge in her eyes slowed, clouded into puzzlement as she watched him. He thought he saw her hands grow less taut on the gun.

'Can you speak?' she said, her rich mouth twisting in contempt.

He drew a deep breath and then shrugged his broad shoulders.

'I don't know what I'm doing here,' he said. 'I don't even know what place this is.'

His heavy face was handsome, strong and humorous, but the lines of it now betrayed a stranger in command of him; a monster within that stole away his character and left him empty of himself.

The oddness of his despair caught her imagination suddenly, and her curiosity grew, as if womanlike she sensed the deep feeling of helplessness in him.

'Where have you come from?' she said, no pity sounding in her voice, only the determination to know.

He brought his cigarettes from his pocket and fumbled one out before he said:

'I'm trying to remember.'

'Are you ill?' she said roughly.

'I'm near it,' he said, and then gave a short mirthless laugh. 'Why do you want to know these things? I thought in a place like this I wouldn't have to answer any questions!'

There was a sudden fury of anger in his voice, and he saw the gun rise slightly in response to his violence.

'Why are you so dead keen to know, anyway?' he said, going towards her. He stopped just short of the gun. 'Why threaten me?'

'I'm looking after myself,' she said, evenly. 'It's lonely round here.'

'I'm not thinking of rape,' he said, turning half away to light the cigarette.

'I don't know what you're thinking,' she said. 'I'm just making sure of what you're doing.' He had dropped the tie to the rock and she glanced at it. 'Were you going to jump in?'

He gave a short, contemptuous laugh. 'Do I look the kind?'

'No. But you can never tell.'

He looked pointedly at the gun. 'You think I'm mad. Is that how it goes?'

'I told you before,' she said, 'it's a lonely place. I don't carry this gun for men, but it can be handy.' Slowly she let the gun barrel slope right down until she held it under her arm, carrying fashion.

He did not even feel relief that a sudden charge of paralysing shot would not now come into his guts. He had feared it during those last moments, because of her hatred of him, but relief it seemed, was a kind of peace that had gone from him, as if death already had its hand upon his soul.

She watched him, and a sudden brightness came into her eyes, almost of pain, as if she read and felt the dreadful feelings stirring in him. She turned away and stepped on to the rutted track.

'Perhaps you're all right,' she said, and turned to face him again.

'I'm all right,' he said, following her. 'It's just now and again I feel I'm going to die.'

His light grey eyes watched her keenly, almost as if challenging her to laugh at him. She looked into his eyes steadily, trying to probe the secrets behind the grey deathliness of their stare, and then suddenly withdrew, as if scared he might read into hers.

'How long have you been like this? You're big. You look strong. What's happened to you?'

'It isn't the body,' he said. He looked down at his big chest, the brown of his powerful forearms, and great wide stride of his legs as he stood there, firm and steady as ever they had been, and he felt a momentary pleasure in possessing that body, and sad that the separation had

16

begun. 'It's in the mind these troubles come.'

'When?'

'It's been gathering,' he said, staring away to the birch woods whispering in the hot sun. 'It's like a disease. There's a little spot you ignore, and then it spreads quietly, spreads and spreads and suddenly there's a blackness all round, everywhere, so you can't even stand back and see it. Suddenly, the blackness is you, not something you had, but you, yourself.'

They began to walk along the rutted path, as if by unspoken consent, until she stopped.

'You've been here before,' she said, her eyes were narrowed in suspicion.

'No,' he said. 'Never.'

She frowned slightly.

'Come back with me,' she said, and went on walking.

He stayed still a pace behind, startled by the unexpected. To him it did not matter if he went with her or stayed; there was nothing left of that importance, but the strangeness of her turn was giving curiosity a rebirth.

'Where are you going?' he asked.

'To the house,' she said.

The house, he thought. There was only one house in all this great wild part, where once the landlord lived, and the landlord died and so had the house and where the boy had played there were only ghosts and shadows of things that lived no more.

'You live here — in this place?' he said. But you can't, he thought. It was mine, all this, years ago, the only place that ever was mine. It was my life, the little boy I was; the little boy I kicked from my life and choked and then was sorry.

She saw him wipe his face with a handkerchief.

'You thought of something,' she said, bitterly. 'It frightened you again.'

'Yes.' He drew a long breath. 'I felt I was lost.'

'Aren't you lost?'

'Yes. I didn't mean that way.'

'I don't believe you would have gone in the lake.'

He did not speak. She walked on slowly along the rutted lane, watching her sandals, bringing little spurts of sand forward with the swing of her foot.

The track joined to the overgrown gravel of an old drive and she swung to the right. His step faltered as he saw the lodge, its plaster fallen and patched standing by the old gate with the creeper winding through its ironwork. She turned momentarily towards him as he hesitated and her eyes grew bright with suspicion and anger.

She tossed her head and went to the doorway of the lodge where the door itself stood open, as it had done the many years before as he remembered.

She went into the little room where long ago the servant had sat waiting his duty. Plaster had fallen and the fireplace was brown with rust, but even now, faded on the walls and streaked with damp stood the pencil and crude paint of his 'secret' maps and messages.

'You remember this,' she said, turning to him with a challenge.

He shook his head.

'What is it?' he asked. 'You don't live here?'

Her mouth twisted into a contemptuous smile. She brushed past him, out into the sunlight again. He followed her along the great curve of the old drive, heavily tufted with grass and patched with mould. The bushes had grown on either side, trying to join across the space between them. It had grown like a jungle, and the oppression of the gathering evergreens about them gave him a sudden feeling of being stifled. He caught her arm and pressed it to his side. She turned her head quickly and looked directly into his eyes and saw the fear there. She kept walking, looking ahead again. He let her arm go.

They broke into the view of the house, the great white front, lines of windows staring blindly at the sky, stained and grimy now, like an unshaven man, but still noble, somehow inspiring in a way that held his breath. And he remembered how he had come here so often and watched, breathless and afraid, and filled with the great emotion of ambition. 'One day I will come back and have this house, when I have been round the world and found treasure.' He could hear his childish, excited whisper again, and suddenly feeling welled up in him so that he wanted to cry.

But if he cried, she would know.

She went ahead to the great broad steps, went up one, then turned and faced him. He stopped, scared of the directness in her stare.

'It's a big house,' he said, looking to the windows ranged out along one side, then the other. 'Is this where you live?'

And then with the re-awakening of emotions in him he thought, What is she doing here? Here in *my* house? How can she live here, among the weeds and the choking jungle.

She went ahead again, and he knew she had turned to try and catch his expression.

One great leaf of the doors was open. She went into the hall, the old-panelled place with the yawning throat of a stone fireplace, and stood the gun against the panels in a corner. He had been in here, heart beating like a dozen hammers, stiff with the thrill of adventure. He felt the excitement of those dead moments brush him again, and the greyness of despair faded from his eyes, leaving a light growing there.

Then as feelings reawoke, he saw her there, facing him again, her features, her roundness, the whole desirable body of her moving in his sight like reality growing from the flatness of a picture, catching his senses in a sexual aura. The remembered scene about her faded into shadow as the sight of her increased in radiance in his mind. The curl of anger and hatred still showed in her lips, yet it raised in him only a responsive heat to change it. He saw her rich bosom and it drew him with the same feeling of that strange despairing desire to go back into the dream. To him she had twisted in his mind and become the reality of escape, the arms of new life.

She saw the growing warmth of his look and knew it. She kept her eyes steadily on him, daring him, the twisting of her lips growing slightly different, into knowledge of power and sureness of her sex. Yet in her eyes there grew a light that was not plain curiosity, but something deeper, probing her own thoughts as well as his.

Now in the sudden pulsating elation of escape he was blind to every sense but those she stirred in him.

'You know this place,' she said.

'It's you I seem to know,' he said huskily.

'You never saw me before,' she said.

He shook his head. 'I don't remember. It's a feeling.'

'Where did you come from?' she said.

He shook his head and shrugged. She turned away and went through a door he knew would lead to the great kitchen, where once he had hid in a vast oven fearing the noise of wind blowing a door that had been a man coming to find him. Her sandals slapped on the flags. She went to a table by the window and poured a drink from a bottle of brandy.

'This'll help,' she said, holding out the glass.

He came and took it, deliberately

touching her hand, as if it was something he must do. The urge in him to touch her went in that moment almost beyond control, but sense came through his fingers on the cold glass and he almost crushed it. She watched him, narrow-eyed as if she knew his feelings. He drank with a clumsy gulp, and the fire sank into his belly, catching his breath.

'Why don't you remember?' she said.

'Because I don't want to!' he cried suddenly. 'I'm trying to get away from it, not back into it. Why must you know? What does it matter to you?' He thumped the glass on the table and turned away as if ashamed of his outburst.

'You're running away,' she said, coming closer behind him. 'All right. I know that. It's obvious to anybody. But why do you come here? Of all places in the world, why this one?'

He turned back, his mouth twisted in a sneer.

'Because in some dream I saw a beautiful woman standing here, waiting for me, a bosom I could sink into and forget.'

She searched his eyes for a moment, then laughed shortly.

'You're crazy,' she said.

'I've been telling you that,' he said. 'I've been explaining it in the only way I can without frightening myself.'

'You must have a name,' she said.

'You, too,' he answered. 'I'll swop. Allison.'

Her eyes narrowed again in doubt.

'All right. Kate.'

He sat on the edge of the big table, his head hanging to his chest. The drowsiness of many sleepless nights was claiming him. It weighed his eyelids down, making sleep he could not resist.

Once the idea swam into his mind that there had been something in the brandy, but it dissipated in the growing cloud of peace claiming his mind. He half turned and lay down on the table, then lay flat on his back.

She watched patiently, without surprise. In a minute or more she went to him, took his arm and shook it. There was no response. He stayed still but for the deep, regular moving of his chest.

Carefully, slowly she searched his pockets. She found cigarettes, a lighter, loose change and that was all.

She stood back, watched him for a while longer then went out into the hall and took the gun. She went out on to the steps and the heat of the midday sun struck her, and made her realise she felt a heat, perhaps of excitement as well as summer. She unfastened her shirt, pulled it out of her jeans and flapped it gently until she felt cool air on her bare skin, letting the gun rest between her legs. She took it up again and walked quickly away along the overgrown drive, past the lodge and into the rutted track again. She went quickly along until she saw the great anvil of the rock overhanging the lake, then she turned off the track and went down into the wood.

She ran with long strides, her shirt flying open, showing the richness of her breasts, brown from many suns, until she came near the car. She stopped a little way off and watched it as if it might suddenly come alive. She looked all round, but she was alone in the wood,

26

and there were only the birds and the faint shivering of the little trees to hear.

She went to the car, opened the door and laid the gun on the floor at the back. Then she looked in and picked up the jacket. She searched the pockets but found only a silver pencil, two fresh-laundered handkerchiefs, and a tab in the pocket showing it to be a fashionable lightweight, tailored in Bond Street with the customer's name, 'C. E. Allison.' She considered the name for a moment, as if testing the truth of it, then she got into the driving seat and opened the dash cupboard. There was a bottle of Cologne, a road book, two more packets of cigarettes unbroken. There was nothing else in the door pockets but maps, unmarked though worn.

She saw the wallet, which had fallen to the floor and picked it up. It was soft and had gold initials, C.E.A. She found nothing in it but money. Curiously, she counted out twenty-two fives and seven ones, then put the notes back and slipped the wallet into the hip pocket of her jeans. She sat for a moment looking round the car, then looked at the dash, turned the key and started the engine. It was going, the oil was up, the lights went out when she dipped the accelerator.

She sat with the engine idling, staring through the windscreen, then she shifted the lever to R and began to back the big car up the leaf-strewn slope the way it had come. The only sounds were the hushing of dead vegetation under the wheels and the rustling of little branches brushed aside. She came up to the top and swung backwards on to the track, stopping violently as the rear overhung the drop off the edge into the lake. She went forward on over the ruts and stopped by the rock.

The tie lay there, like a waiting snake on the hot rock. She got out and picked it up, then looked carefully round, as if something more might be there, but she saw nothing and got back into the car again. She drove past the lodge, between the clawing bushes of the overgrown drive and round the corner of the house into the stable yard. She drove on into the shadowy inside of a stall row, then stopped and got out. She went to go, then returned to the car and took the keys out of the ignition lock. She went round, unlocked the boot and opened it. It was empty.

If the man had come a long way, he had come with no luggage.

She closed the boot again and slipped the keys into her pocket with the wallet. Then she walked slowly out into the sun.

★ ★ ★

He still slept, his legs hanging over the table edge from his knees. She watched him for a while, as if in sleep there might be some tell-tale that would tell her things.

'Allison, Allison,' she said, testing again.

She shook her head and went into the hall. The heat of the sun was growing in the house. Her passing through had disturbed him, and she heard water running in the kitchen. She looked back a moment, then sat down astride the arm of a big wing chair, her hands in the front pockets of her jeans, and waited. For a moment she took her hands and put them to fasten her shirt again, then dropped them and waited in the same position as before.

When he came into the hall he looked better. The leadenness had gone from his grey eyes, and his body moved more lightly.

'Sleep well?' Her mouth twisted scornfully as she asked the question.

He looked at her and at the gap of brown skin and the curves showing beneath the open shirt.

'You laced that brandy,' he said, putting his tongue round his mouth. 'Tastes like a sick aspirin.'

'Sleeping draught,' she said. 'It's harmless, and you needed it.'

He went to the open door and looked out at the overgrown drive, shimmering in the sun.

'I can hardly remember what happened,' he said, turning back. 'Did you say your name was Kate?'

'You couldn't remember anything

before, either,' she said.

'No.' He got his cigarettes out. 'Funny place I've come to. Kind of drives everything else out of my mind. Greeted with a gun and invited home to a sick drink. What next?'

'It's not all one-sided,' she said, shifting slightly on the chair arm. 'You were going to jump in the lake, but you changed your mind without much persuasion.'

'You're plenty of persuasion,' he said, lighting a cigarette, 'even for a man temporarily insane.'

'You just meant to make it look as if you'd jumped in the lake.' She reached out, took the cigarette from his fingers and began to smoke it. 'How did you know there was a lake, anyway. It's three miles off any road. Sort of a lucky wrong turning, wasn't it?'

He looked out of the door again, then back at her with an almost sly swiftness.

'What are you doing here?' he asked. 'You said you were alone. Why here, in a place like this? Remote, lonely.'

'Weren't you hoping to be lonely, too?' She almost smiled.

31

He ignored the question.

'The place must have been empty for years before you came,' he said, and flicked the top edge of a wing chair. 'And this stuff — was it here before?' He knew it had been, for he could remember the inexplicable mystery of the chairs and sofas and tables covered up like ghosts all those years ago. Things that nobody wanted; as if the people who had lived there had suddenly vanished leaving everything just as it was, even the coffee to get cold on the stove. There had been a strange quality of richness in the desertion he remembered; it had been that queer lushness which had made him determine to have this place, so long ago.

'I took it, like this,' she said.

'What do you *do*?' he queried.

'Shoot,' she said.

'Why did you bring me back here?'

'I wanted to know why you came.'

'What does it matter to you if anyone comes?'

She shrugged. 'I like to know.'

They looked at each other, searching

for answers to their mysteries but found only the certain existence of sexual magnetism.

He went closer to her, watching her as his body awakened. She looked at him steadily, knowing what he was thinking, and staying quite still where she sat.

'I'll admit something,' he said, abruptly. 'I knew this place many years ago. When I was a child.'

'I knew,' she said. 'You wouldn't have come here without knowing it.'

She was quite firm in that she had never believed his lie, her continued pressure on the point had won.

'It's no guilty secret,' he said.

Her eyes became suddenly pinpointed and almost luminous.

'Is there anyone following you?' she asked very slowly and clearly.

'No,' he said.

The brilliance of suspicion changed into a puzzled light, and for a moment he thought she would ask another question, but she shrugged very slightly and looked away from him.

'I remember this whole place,' he

said, turning away. 'The long corridor here — '

He crossed the big hall and opened a door. There was a passage beyond. On one side there were doors, still, but on the other, only the broken remnants of the walls, with laths, like broken ribs pricking the sky and rubble and cement strewn idly on the once spacious corridor. It was like a film set, where one stepped through a door straight into the garden. He looked back at her, shocked.

'It fell down,' she said. 'I think that will happen to the rest of it.'

'It couldn't have done!' he protested. 'It was built like a castle!'

'But it did,' she said coolly.

He looked back at the devastation through the open doorway and had the vague feeling of watching the ruin of some overwhelming ambition. Panic as he had felt in dreams flooded in him suddenly, almost as if he could feel reality slipping away like spilling sand from his terrified fists.

As he turned back to her she stood up.

'What's the matter?' she snapped.

He slammed the door shut and turned back to her.

'It's part of the madness,' he said breathlessly. 'Sudden feelings that everything has gone — '

'But you're not alone now,' she said, watching him as he stopped before her.

'No.' His voice was husky, little more than a whisper. Suddenly he put his hands on her shoulders and pulled her to him, bringing the challenge in her eyes close to his own.

Something grabbed his shoulder and swung him round, off his balance. He let her go and as his head twisted round he saw a man's face, and shooting, it seemed from out of it, a savage fist.

His head was knocked back, his knees faltered. He went staggering back against the panelling, and collapsed in a heap to the floor. He shook his head and hauled himself up to his feet by clinging to a table. He saw the man standing in front of him, feet apart, fists ready, threatening, but Allison did nothing to defend himself. He grinned as if in some savage pleasure with the pain. The man came at him again, and he did nothing, but stood, fatalistic, uncaring. The man hit him twice in a fury of temper and spite and he went down and rolled over, still but for the gasping of his big chest.

The girl looked down at him, then to the man. Slowly she fastened the front of her shirt, and then with a twisted little smile of contempt, she turned away.

The man gripped her arm and swung her round to him, his dark face lowering, white with anger and jealousy. Before he could speak she ground the burning end of her cigarette into the back of his hand and he snatched it away from her arm.

'What good do you think that's going to do?' Her voice hissed with a venom that showed in her blazing eyes.

It held the man still for a moment.

2

Allison felt no real pain, just a stiffness in his face. He could hear a man speaking to him, and he looked up. He was slumped into the sofa by the refectory table. Surprisingly, it seemed, the sun still streamed in at the great open door.

'I thought you were going for her,' the man said, peering down at him.

Allison looked into the heavy, dark features, the sullen brown eyes, glowing now with the reflected light from the door. He had not shaved and his chin was growing blue. Allison could smell the sweat on him, and sat forward suddenly shoving him away like a man wanting air.

'Going for her?' he said, and ran a hand round his face.

'Attacking her,' the man said. 'That's what it looked like. I'm sorry.'

'You didn't seem to be sorry at the time,' Allison said. 'I should have kicked

37

you right in the belly.'

'You didn't do anything — nothing at all,' the man said, watching him intently.

'I think I enjoyed it,' Allison said. 'A masochist.'

'You have to be careful, these lonely places, with a woman,' the man said in broken sentences. He shoved his hands into the pockets of his slacks and turned away. 'It's off the beaten track. It's a bit startling when you suddenly find somebody's here.'

'Shouldn't be guilty,' Allison said, and got up.

The man turned to him suddenly, would have spoken, but staring changed his mind.

'I don't get your attitude,' Allison persisted. 'That girl doped me. You knocked me out. What the hell are you scared of?'

'We just like to be alone,' the man said, and grinned.

'I don't think it's a honeymoon,' Allison said. He got out his cigarettes and worked his jaw to overcome the stiffness he felt.

'That wasn't dope,' the man said, temporarily eager to explain. 'It's a sleeping draught I take. It was just that she was frightened being alone with a stranger.'

Allison remembered her sharply.

'She didn't strike me as being the frightened sort,' he said.

'First impressions aren't always right,' the man said.

Allison lit his cigarette, went to the door and looked out into the hot sunlight. He went down the steps on to the neglected gravel, then turned and looked up at the house. The man came to the top of the steps, watching.

'You knew the place,' he said.

'She told you?' Allison stayed looking upwards to the roof line. 'I can't make out how it fell down. The front's all right. You'd never know, would you?'

'These old places — they go rotten,' the man said.

'I knew it well,' Allison said. 'Do you mind if I look?'

The man hesitated, then :

'Okay — if you feel like it.' He turned

39

back to the door as Allison came slowly up the steps. 'She didn't know that stuff was in the brandy. I was bad last night. There was only a small drop in the bottle. I shoved it in and was going to take it to bed, but I went out instead.'

Allison said nothing.

'When you get a bad night, you can only dope it off or walk it off,' the man said.

'I've had some,' Allison said, and the grey-edged shadows of his followers moved in on him again. He felt his jaw to bring himself away from them and back to the immediate present.

As they came back into the hall Allison pointed to the door on the right of the panelled room.

'The stairs,' he said. 'Do they still go up?'

The man looked at him, then nodded. Allison opened the door and went through to the broad old stairs and up to the great landing, big as three rooms. A far wall had gone. The frayed edges of laths and broken wood framed the scene of the wild garden. Stretching beyond the fallen wall of the west wing tumbled on the bushes and great high weeds of the jungle below them. Beyond the solitary sentinel of a chimney stack he saw the sea sparkling in the valley between the hills.

'Just collapsed,' the man said.

'Should never have thought it could have done,' Allison said, and looked at his companion. 'What are the owners going to do?'

The man shrugged.

'It isn't worth doing anything,' he said. 'These big, old places. If the Government don't want 'em for offices, what else can you do with them?'

Allison knew the man was hedging at everything, but he had not prepared any lies. It would be easy to trip him up, but that would not necessarily get at the truth, and Allison, as a recreation to his own worries, was suddenly interested in the truth of this place, and this ill-matched couple.

'Do the owners know you're here?' Allison asked sharply.

The man stared and then began to laugh.

41

'No,' he said. 'Nobody knows but you.'

'Don't you think you might share a confidence, then?'

'I don't particularly want to,' he answered.

'What about Kate?'

The man's smile faded.

'Kate's with me,' he said.

'All right,' Allison said. 'But if I go, then I could tell everybody you're here.'

'That's okay,' said the man, slowly. 'You're not going.'

Allison spun his cigarette out and watched it arc down into the rubble below the gaping hole in the wall.

★ ★ ★

Allison's automatic reaction to the man's statement was to go at once, to challenge the assurance the man had in his own ability to hold him there.

But there were two factors that made him pause, and one sprang in relief from the other. He wanted to hide as much as they did and trying to forget what he was hiding from needed an engagement for his mind, and that engagement was here. There was a strange personal anger against the people who had wrecked the house, the one ambition that through all dreams and disasters had been the last refuge of hope. A shattered wreck now, with only a part left to live in; a monstrous deformation that no one now would want.

It was almost as if some friend had been shattered by a great explosion, and stood maimed and pitiful.

He turned to the man suddenly.

'All right,' he said. 'I've no wish to go.'

The man gave a brief smile, as if relieved at the turnout of the stranger's decision.

'We could agree, then, not to ask questions,' the man said.

'We could, but we wouldn't stick to it,' Allison said. 'You can't kill curiosity by agreement.'

The man watched him.

'Okay. Then we know what to expect,' he said.

He turned and went away down the stairs. Allison remained in the queer silence of the place, the man's departure leaving him oddly at a loss.

He went to the great gap and looked out along the fallen bastion of the wall, the curious up-jags of wood, like broken bones through flesh, the desperate determination of the weeds to force through the sudden avalanche which had buried them in heaps of dust and brick, the tottering shapes of furniture staring dumbly from the debris, like old prostitutes still hoping to attract a passerby.

Birds sang in the trees, and the leaves hushed gently. There were no other sounds of life in the place. And standing there on the very brink of the disaster he had the odd breathless feeling of climbing a tottering house in the dream, being forced on and up into greater danger because there was now no way down.

He could not understand why he should think there must be some mystery about this collapse, unless it was born of some innate refusal to admit defeat of a childhood belief. Houses could fall down —

But not this one. Surely never this one?

But if it had not fallen, how had it been destroyed? Why? Had those two come to this place with a malicious, lunatic determination to destroy the place, piece by piece? What kind of savage desire could that satisfy? Yet what sane reason could anyone have for such a deed?

But then, they had not acted sanely, these two. One incident after another had been violent and ill-thought —

But what else had his headlong, senseless flight been but a race along the edge of sanity. He saw himself suddenly racing through the early day, like a wasp trying to escape from an empty jam-jar. The return to a dream place, the hiding the car, the preparations —

Surely only the girl coming had stopped him on the verge of complete insanity? Would anyone have believed the story of a suicide?

He stood there like someone staring at another man, judging, trying to understand and growing more remote from the image of his mad self as each action was replayed in his memory.

He turned from it, horrified and sick with the realisation. Memory retreated. The atmosphere of the old, half-wrecked place gripped him again and he looked at the walls of the landing on which he stood. Great cracks lined it, the gaping caries of decay exposed by the part-collapse showed the weakness that had been hidden.

'If some fell,' he said, 'then the rest might go, too.'

He looked at the starred, cracked ceiling, the great holes in the old plaster, pieces hanging from it by hairs. Slowly he crossed the floor to the door to the east wing bedrooms. It was partly open. He went through. The corridor beyond seemed to be as he remembered it, with no cracks showing in the ceiling, but the wall above the panelling near the door had an ominous crack, as if the east part was being gradually torn away.

He walked slowly along the silent place, subconsciously searching, though the spur was only distrust. He looked into two rooms, and found them as he had seen them years ago, sheet-covered, their off-white now grey, but they smelt fresh and dust had been taken off. Further on the ages of neglect remained. He opened three doors where a forest of webs hung like curtains and such old furniture as was scattered about was seen only dimly through the confusion. The difference between these rooms and the others was startling. No one could have cleaned such rooms in a short time, they must have been in use for quite a while.

He turned back and hurried to the landing, and once more looked keenly down through the rubble, and the jagged edges of the still-standing parts of the walls.

'What are you looking for?'

He swung round and saw the girl standing near the wall where the stairs went down. He must have passed her as he had come in, for he had not heard her approach. She came slowly towards him, the beginning of a smile on her lips.

'What are you looking for?' she repeated.

'Cobwebs,' he said.

She stopped, her feet apart, her hands resting on her hips.

'It's too late to find them down there,' she said, curiously. 'Why does it hurt you so?'

'It seems like a part of my childhood gone away.'

'How long since you were here?'

'I was fourteen when we went from here. Twenty years.'

'You didn't live here, did you?' She seemed to come closer to him.

'No. We lived in Wendon village. I used to walk over here or use a bike.'

'By yourself?'

'Usually.'

'Nobody lived here then?'

'Nobody. I only once saw anybody. I think it was a poacher.'

'You used to get in here?'

He nodded. 'There was a broken window at the back. That was the secret way in. When I first came in with another boy, I was frightened of

48

the furniture under those sheets. I used to think they were queer sort of people, jumbo size. Once a storm came. It got very dark and the lightning flashed like the devil. I remember running through the rooms in panic, the lightning strikes making the chairs seem to be running after me, coming closer with each flash. It was the sort of hopeless, panicky running away one does in a dream.'

'And no one lived here?'

'To me it always seemed the whole place was waiting for someone to come back,' he said. 'I realise now that someone must have come in fairly regularly to sweep and clean because it wasn't dirty, as I remember.'

'Did you explore it?' She cocked her head on one side, and in him memory receded before a sharp awareness of her. He hesitated before he answered.

'Yes,' he said, and walked slowly past her to the doorway again. He stared down the wide corridor as she followed him. 'But some rooms were locked,' he said, and now that she was behind him he remembered again. 'There was a high carver in the dining-room. I used to sit there and think I was king, and all empty chairs around the table were my knights . . . '

'You sound like an old man,' she said. 'Like someone remembering because he knows he's going to die.'

He turned to her.

'Perhaps I'm dead already,' he said, bitterly. 'That boy has gone, and the adventure and the excitement that he had died with him. I came back, not just to remember, but to feel if I was really dead.'

'Would you have gone into the lake?'

He looked at her and then suddenly smiled.

'No,' he said. 'When I came back into this house everything changed. Not immediately, but gradually. I can feel the old magic working now. It's changed. It's not so big as I thought it was, but the smell's the same, the very feeling of excitement is moving again. It's mine, as it was before. I could murder the fool who blew it up!'

She stared. Her eyes were cold with a

light like splintered ice.

'It fell down,' she said.

He looked surprised to find that she had said it.

'Your man said that,' he commented, and touched his jaw. 'A quick-tempered soul. Who is he?'

'Franz,' the girl said, and shrugged. 'He doesn't matter.'

'A foreigner? He didn't sound like it.'

'It's just a name,' she said casually, and looked around her.

'But who's he?' Allison said. 'He didn't like me.'

'You don't have to worry about him,' she said.

'So you're with him in trying to stop me being curious,' he said. 'I told Franz, it won't work.'

She laughed quietly, and it made him angry. He turned away from her and went into a big bedroom looking out over the overgrown garden. The shape of its civilisation could be seen still from this upper view.

It was blown up, he thought. It was

blown up. It couldn't have fallen like that. It was strong, you can see it was strong, the way it tumbled and smashed the furniture, burst the wood, crushed down the little trees and the tough bushes. It was too strong to fall. It was blown up.

How?

He sensed her close behind him.

'Why are you so worried about this house?' she said. 'It was only a place you knew years ago. What does it matter?'

'It's just something I've got to know,' he said, sharply. 'I'm like that. I get the Big Urge to know something, and it doesn't stop until I do know. I've always been like that, until lately — '

'What happened lately?'

'I got frightened to know,' he said. 'I started backing away from things, trying to pretend they hadn't happened, that other things couldn't happen because I refused to know what had already happened. Everything was starting to go wrong . . . '

'Bad luck?' she said softly.

He shook his head.

'Bad me,' he said. 'I didn't know that till I got back here. I tried to think it was bad luck, got sorry for myself, blamed everything but me. That's how you get. Frightened to meet people, just hiding yourself, It's a disease. One of those you think can never happen to you. Half the time when you're thinking that, it's happening to you, but you can't see it. I couldn't. I ran back here, not knowing very clearly what I meant to do. You could almost say it was subconscious, when you first fall in the water some instinct makes you try to swim . . . Then the lake. When I saw it, something changed in me, but I didn't see what it was. I thought the boy was dead. I came to cry over him. It was like that. But the lake, and the house got hold of me as they always did. The boy was alive all right. I could see him, hear him, know what he was thinking and feeling, and then suddenly I was inside him again. It was like a bright shock, seeing myself as I am now. I knew then it wasn't the boy who was dead. Nothing could ever kill the spirit. It was the man trying to strangle himself.'

His eyes were alive with a light she had not seen before. The heaviness of the grey mood in his face had gone.

'You've suffered,' she said.

He almost laughed.

'I made myself,' he answered.

He looked down through the window again. Directly ahead he looked over a floor of trees, almost level, it seemed, stretching to the sea sparkling under the hot sun. Below he saw the foreshortened Franz come out from the main door and stop. Franz looked at his watch, then stared around him.

'Expecting somebody?' Allison said.

She came and looked down.

'There is no one to come,' she said, watching the man below. 'Your curiosity will make you imagine things.'

'All right,' he said, turning to her, eyes narrowed.

'But who is Franz — to you?'

'It doesn't matter,' she said, watching him.

'Perhaps it does,' he said. 'Perhaps I

like you. I would want to know who Franz was.'

'How would that make any difference to you? If you like me, you know what to do.' There was the soft beginning of a smile on her face as she watched him.

'Franz was very cross when I touched you.'

She pouted and looked angry for an instant.

'He imagines himself to be more important than he is,' she said. 'That's all that's the matter with him.' She touched his arm, feeling it beneath the shirt. 'I'm sure you could show him where he belongs.'

She stood against him and lifted her face, lips faintly smiling, the challenge in her eyes bright and sure. He put his arms round her, slowly and felt her body tighten against his. The attraction that had radiated between them now locked into a real sensation, and the play was suddenly gone in fire. They kissed with passion as if they had known each other before. As their lips parted she laughed at him in faint scorn.

'Franz,' she said huskily. 'Who is Franz?'

They laughed together, sharing. He pulled the shirt off her shoulder and kissed her sun-browned flesh.

'Tell me about this boy,' she said. 'More. I want to know him.'

He raised his head again.

'He was always dreaming of beautiful princesses that had to be rescued from these rooms,' he said. 'He had his knights, but they all got cut down by the defenders, and he always had to fight his way up alone.'

She brushed his lips with hers then drew her head back.

'Where did he come from?' she said. 'Where did he go to?'

'He only came to life when he was here,' he said. 'Just as he is now.'

She laughed softly and pushed him away, then pulled her shirt back over her shoulder.

'Franz is coming upstairs,' she said.

He looked quickly down through the window. Franz had gone. When he turned back to her she had gone to the open door of the room.

Who in hell is Franz? he wondered as he followed her.

Franz appeared in the doorway.

'Time we ate,' he said.

She agreed almost as if obeying an order.

Franz had laid places in the kitchen, and there was a smell of some rich cooking when he opened the door of the big, white oven. He brought out a big tureen that smelt of game soup, and when he set it on the table and took the lid of Allison became struck with a hunger that was a sharp pang. Franz took a cloth and pulled a loaf of bread he had baked out of another oven. Then he put that on the table and fetched a bottle of port and sloshed the wine liberally into the soup.

He's not English, Allison thought, though he speaks so well.

He sat down, watching the meal come up as Franz served it, and saw Kate sitting there watching him with brief, mischievous glances, and suddenly he felt sorry for the dark, sullen man standing there; sorry that he was being cheated.

Allison had the sudden senseless urge to beat her by saying, 'She's cheating you, Franz: she wants me behind your back.'

He took up the long bread and broke a piece off as if he was breaking a person, and the devilish urge to hurt faded back into himself.

Franz's soup was magnificent.

'Never thought I'd take to soup on a hot day,' Allison said. 'You're a genius, Franz.'

'I'm glad you liked it,' Franz said. 'I was frightened the sleeping draught had spoiled your appetite.'

His dark eyes slid slyly from Allison to the girl. Kate might not have heard except for a faint smile as she broke bread.

Again the regret for Franz stole over Allison, then he looked at the girl, and the flood of desire that came over him drowned any feeling for Franz. He got up abruptly and went out of the room.

Franz watched the open door where he

had gone, then his dark gaze drifted back to Kate. He raised his thick, black brows in query.

'He doesn't know anything at all,' Kate said in a voice that carried only to Franz.

'Then why did he come?'

'Sentiment. A childhood place.' She looked sulky at being questioned.

'I don't believe that,' Franz said. 'He is here for something. You had better go on finding out.'

She shrugged and toyed with a piece of bread.

'All right,' she said, but seemed reluctant.

'You should watch him,' Franz warned.

She became angry quite suddenly.

'He won't go,' she hissed. 'I keep telling you, it's sentiment. He came to find it. He won't go till he has.'

'He's chasing a ghost?'

'If you like. Yes.'

★ ★ ★

Allison opened the door to the ruined passage, and this time, went in, stepping amongst rubble, staring over the tumbled sea of wreckage as if here might lie the answer to the mystery of the disaster. But save for the rocky peaks of furniture which had proved too strong, all had been covered by the expanse of the collapse. The slates, torn lead strips from the gutter, the queer lattice of ripped laths, the cobwebbed frames of the joists, the tumbled, mortar-dusty masses of brickwork, still holding together in defiance of the devastation.

And then in the midst of the crazy mess he saw something that was by nature different from the vast mixture of the rest. It caught his senses as scent tickles a dog's nose. His eyes on the curious object he picked and trod his way carefully amid the rubbish until he came far along the corridor and could look back towards the door through which he had come.

The object was now like some queer white animal peering out from beneath a great sloping mass of joists, bricks and scattered slates. With a sick shock he recognised it as a human hand, and behind it, like a mad tombstone, the back of a great carved chair struck up through the broken remains of the upper floors.

He looked up at the door through which he had come and saw the girl standing in the opening.

'You won't give in, will you?' she said. Her voice carried clearly in the humming heat of the afternoon.

He hesitated, then picked his way back through the dangerous wreckage.

'No,' he said, as he reached her. 'I came so near to giving in this morning I think it's a weakness I'll try and forget.'

They came into the hall.

'Were you here when the place collapsed?' he asked.

'We were away then,' she said.

'You and Franz?'

'Me and Franz. Yes.'

They watched each other for a moment, searching.

'He's a good cook,' Allison said, and turned towards the main door.

★ ★ ★

61

Franz stood by the stable door where the Bentley was. He seemed to have no need to search it, but stood thinking and smoking a small cigar.

'Eight thousand sterling,' he murmured thoughtfully, then moved round and looked at the number plate at the rear. 'Why? Why run away?'

He pulled a very small automatic pistol from the pocket just below his belt, and then from his left-hand pocket brought a handful of bullets. He dropped one or two as he filled the magazine but left them on the hay-strewn floor until he had finished, then he put the little gun back into his belt pocket and picked up the ammunition.

He went out of the stable into the bright sunlight and halted again looking at the side of the house, his frown pained somehow as well as puzzled.

He walked slowly round the house to the front, and stopped as he saw Allison under a monkey tail tree, staring up at the house front. Allison saw him. Franz let his shoulders relax and went slowly to the blond man.

'You knew the place well,' Franz said.

'I told you,' Allison said shortly.

'And yet still you are trying to find out something about it,' Franz went on. 'What is it that you can find now that wasn't here before?'

'Maybe you could answer that question.'

'I am here, peaceably living,' Franz said. 'I am a very ordinary man. It was offered to me if I would take care of it, but — '

'A caretaker!' Allison said, startled by the simplicity of the explanation.

' — but it seems I really came too late,' Franz went on. 'The fabric is rotten.'

'The house was years without a caretaker — '

'Ah, no. There was always someone,' Franz said. 'Someone who came in from a village. But he died.'

'When did he die?'

Franz watched him sharply for a moment, then began to smile very slowly. 'I don't know,' he said.

Allison lit a cigarette. Yes, there had always been someone. There had never been real dirt, real neglect.

'Who does it belong to — this place?'
he asked.

Franz shrugged.

'I was employed by agents. I answer
to them.'

The ease with which the explanations
seemed to fit had the frustrating effect of
drifting against one's will in a dream.

'Does anyone ever come?' he said,
almost desperate to force a way into
reality.

'No one comes,' Franz said. 'But one
day, someone must. Otherwise why do
we look after it?'

'No one has ever come since you were
here?'

Franz shook his head. He did not
seem to mind answering the questions
now.

'But there must be tradesmen?'

'No one. It is not worthwhile to come
all this way off the road. I bake bread.
There is plenty of wild life. What else we
want we fetch in the Landrover.'

'How long have you been here?'

'Oh — ' Franz looked at the ground,
' — three months.'

Allison wanted to know who Kate was to this man, but suddenly scared away from the question, as if desperate to know, he feared the knowledge.

'The beautiful car — ' Franz said, his eyes glinting slyly. He paused to let the shock jerk Allison round to look at him. 'Kate put it in the stables.'

'Kate?' Allison felt lost, helpless, as if somehow this unexpected act tied him even tighter to this strange atmosphere of unreality.

Franz laughed shortly.

'She found it in the wood. It was a pity to leave it, so she brought it here and shut it up. Now nobody will see it.' He puffed at his little cigar. 'It's worth a lot of money.'

'Not enough,' Allison said laconically. He saw Franz idly feeling the shape of the pistol in the belt pocket, like a man feeling reassured to feel his money was still there. 'What have you done about getting the break shored up? You know it could make the rest collapse if you don't do something to prop it.'

'Everything is being done that is

necessary,' Franz said. 'Of course, you are not used to it yet. Wounds look worse in the bright sun. Blood never looks real. It's too red. It's the sort of colour you dream about. You think blood should be more circumspect, more polite, a more serious colour, not a grand guignol vermilion like it is.'

'What makes you think of blood?' Suddenly the hand from the wreckage seemed to come to life and reach out towards him.

'The rabbits, the hedgehogs, the rats one sees run over in the road,' said Franz. 'That's what I mean. Their blood always seems too bright, but ours is just the same. I like eating animals, but I am sorry for them when they die.'

'When did the wing collapse?'

'It was ten days back.'

'And no one's ever been here?'

Franz shook his head. 'No.'

'Would you know if they had?' Allison snapped.

'I would know,' said Franz.

'Yet you were here when the wing collapsed?'

'I was here.' Franz watched him darkly, steadily. 'Why are you so intent, when you have trouble of your own?'

Allison shrugged and turned away. Franz watched him go, a slow smile on his dark face.

Why didn't I say about the hand? Allison thought. But I didn't mean to. From the very moment when she saw me there, I knew I wouldn't say anything about it until I knew how it got there. Because one moment it's real and horrifying; the next it wavers in the haze of a dream. Shock does that. Perhaps it was a shock to see it there. Was it death in the fall? Was it murder?

Suddenly he knew he meant deep inside him to keep it quiet because of the girl, but he could not see why, or refuse to recognise that she was the keeper of a murder.

For if she and Franz were guardians of a crime, the whole of their strange actions were explained.

And explanation made the mystery

deeper for him, though no curiosity overcame the girl's attraction for him. It was that which was biasing his thoughts. He knew it, and did nothing about it.

3

Through the heat of the afternoon, Allison wandered aimlessly it seemed. Franz watched him, sometimes from a distance, sometimes actually following him. Allison ignored this attention, but when anger rose in him, turned it to thinking of ways to shake the watchdog when he would want to.

Kate did not watch. She knew Allison would not go, and she laughed behind Franz's back.

At about five, she made tea, and it was then she said:

'I've smashed that damned lamp.'

Franz turned on her as if she had spurred him with a knife.

'How?' He seemed to know which lamp she meant. Allison sensed something unusual, dangerous in the air. He knew there were a dozen lamps or more, great brass things, some of them. They used to be kept in a little room off the main corridor; a room that always smelt of paraffin. One of those more or less could not matter.

'Dropped it,' Kate said sulkily.

Franz went out of the kitchen. She said nothing while he was gone but stared out of the window at the crowding green of the trees in the old garden.

When Franz came back, he said:

'I'll have to go into the town quickly.'

She shrugged. Allison saw the man's face darker than ever with anger. It seemed that the smashing of the lamp was a great matter to Franz, and that girl knew it, and sulked for being at fault.

Franz went out, and soon they heard the Landrover engine. Kate began to laugh quietly.

'It was important?' Allison said, curiously.

'Yes. But it can be mended,' she said. 'I wanted to get rid of him for a couple of hours. I'm sick of the sight of him.'

'I was getting rather tired of him. Like an old dog behind me.'

'He thought you might go.' She pouted and then laughed. 'I'm afraid he can't see

70

under his nose.' She turned and looked at him. He stubbed a cigarette on a plate and went to her. She swung round and went out of the room. He followed. She signalled him to wait and went to the main doorway and not on to the step. She stayed a moment, head cocked, listening, then came back to him.

'He's gone,' she said, with a faint smile.

'You don't trust him,' he said.

'I don't want him to know everything,' she said.

'Is he your husband?' He caught her by the arm and held it so tightly that she winced slightly with the pain.

She laughed and waved the fingers of her left hand close to his nose. There was no ring. He shifted his hands from her arm to her back. She laughed at him, then put her hands to his chest and pushed him away, the action taking him by surprise so that his hold on her was lost. She turned and went through the door to the stairs without looking back at him. He followed her quickly, into the lobby and up the stairs into the bedroom where they had kissed before. Then she turned to him.

'There's a room across the corridor,' she said quickly. 'Wait there and don't make any noise. Keep watching.'

He stayed a moment, then she made a gesture for him to hurry, and he turned and went out across the corridor into the room opposite. Once inside he almost closed the door, and then became still, watching through the crack. He could see her in the bedroom. She was sitting on the window-sill, apparently doing nothing. He looked quickly round the room behind him to make sure that it was empty, her attitude of inactivity making him oddly apprehensive. The whole place was quiet, and yet she sat there waiting.

Then he heard a soft dragging in the corridor outside. It was very faint and the sight of the man creeping into view by the open door was startling. For a moment, Allison did not recognise Franz, almost crouching as he crept to the door.

The girl's cold level gaze was watching

the door and when he saw himself watched, Franz straightened and went into full view of her.

'There is a little part missing,' he said. 'I came back to get it.'

'Walked back?'

He nodded, and turned as if to go on past the room. Then he hesitated.

'Where's the man?' he asked.

She shrugged.

'Why are you always worrying about this man?' she said scornfully. 'He won't go.'

She began polishing her nails. Franz looked at her, hesitating still, then went on. After a minute or more he came back.

'I have it,' he said holding something up. He went past and down the stairs his movements clearly audible now.

Allison opened the door and stepped across the corridor into the other room.

'You knew he was coming back' he said.

'When I listened out the front I couldn't hear the truck.' she said. 'Then I thought perhaps he was using the lamp as an excuse, too.' She looked up at him and laughed.

'Franz looks to me like trouble,' he said.

She stood up, smiling.

'I'm trouble, too,' she said. 'What kind are you?'

'Your kind,' he said, taking her in his arms.

'It's funny how you know,' she said.

'Do you?'

'Yes.'

'So the princess really came?'

'You're a romantic,' she said, her eyes steeling over. 'You mustn't be — not here.'

He bent to kiss her but she put her hands on his chest, resisting.

'He hasn't gone,' she said softly. 'He won't go now. He'll try and mend it himself.'

He looked down through the window.

'Are you scared of Franz?' she asked slyly.

'Yes,' he said. 'But not enough.'

She resisted him sharply.

'It's foolish to risk it,' she said. 'Wait

a little. He gets tired.'

He caught her hand and kissed her fingers as she broke away from him. In the moment as she turned away he caught a glimpse of the little smile, part contemptuous, that he was beginning to recognise as if he had known it all his life. He caught her wrist as anger flooded through him and jerked her back towards him. She smiled, lips trembling on the edge of a laugh, and he let her go.

From below he heard the sound of someone moving, and he stayed still. She watched him, as if trying to see whether he was frightened or not. He looked back at her and smiled.

She began to laugh again, softly.

'Go now,' she said.

He went out and down the stairs. The sounds of Franz at work came from the kitchen, and he went there. Franz was soldering the lamp, and Allison stared as he saw it.

'I use it for night hunting,' Franz said, catching his glance. His dark face challenged Allison to deny it.

'Useful, I suppose,' Allison said, looking

away. 'I haven't seen a signalling lamp since I was a scout.'

'You were a Scout?' Franz said.

'I was a Sea Scout,' Allison said. 'We used to make secret landings in the river and the other side had to spot us.'

'This river?' Franz said.

Allison nodded.

'There are good fish in it,' Franz said.

Allison watched the lamp-mending and remembered the lurking figures of the night, when he and his patrol had rowed silently up the river, hugging the shadowy line of the bank, finding the secret place to land, watching out for the spy patrol trying to catch them. He had been older then, about sixteen.

As he remembered, so an idea came to him about Franz's activity. Something to do with smuggling. It was a good spot, and in summer there was always a mass of yachts like paper boats on the water tilting to the wind. So many that one or two easily got lost.

Smuggling what?

Allison went to the sink and drew a glass of water.

'There is plenty of wine,' Franz said.

'Doesn't matter,' Allison replied, staring out into the twilight of the garden.

'Has she made you a bed?'

'No,' Allison said. 'It doesn't matter. I've slept so badly for months it's a shame to have a bed.'

'Are you married?' Franz said. He put the iron into a tin of flux and sent a hissing spurt of steam into the air.

'No,' Allison said, and sat on the edge of the table. 'I thought we agreed not to ask questions?'

Franz laughed sullenly. 'Like you said, it's no good.'

Allison felt a sudden curl of fear inside him at the darkness of the man's attitude. He felt almost as if he had caught the scent of violence radiating from Franz, and he watched the burning iron uneasily, as if he could feel it on his skin.

'You better ask her to get you a room,' Franz said. 'There will be only blankets.'

'I don't want to push you out,' Allison said.

'Like you, I don't sleep much,' Franz said. 'A sofa is good enough.'

A watchdog, Allison thought, then looked at the Aldis lamp and wondered. The man's hand was shaking slightly as he worked as if some passion in him trembled on the surface. Once again Allison felt an odd pity for him and turned away to stifle it. Impatient to be with Kate again made the stifling easier.

'Are you going hunting when you've mended it?' Allison asked.

Franz did not look up as he answered, 'Yes. When you can't sleep, hunting is very good for the nerves.' He looked up at last. 'But you can't do that in the city. Streets are not the same.'

Allison did not reply. Franz put the iron down, then went into the hall, and Allison heard him call Kate. He listened almost tingling on edge for the sound of her voice replying, but when it came it spoke only one word.

'He'll have that north room,' Franz called, and then came back into the kitchen.

There was a mirror propped up over the sink. Allison, his back to Franz, saw the man's dark face glower at the back of his head and he could almost feel the bitterness of the glance.

Franz went to his lamp, took it up and clacked it.

'Okay now,' he said. He went to a corner and picked up a sleek twenty-two rifle, broke it and squinted down the bore. 'I shall hunt tonight. I've got a feeling it won't do any good trying to rest. There's a moon. It should be a good night.'

It was a trap, Allison thought. Either to catch him with Kate, as he had tried before, or to lead him on to trying to find out more about the hand in the debris.

Allison was surprised that he had no human feeling about the hand, or whose it might have been. He felt almost a grievance against it, as if it had been the wrecker of his house. But he did want to know why it was there, how it had got there, why Franz was guarding it. Franz; not Kate as well. Allison refused to bring her into it, letting suspicion be overcome

79

by the warmth of desire.

Silently he measured himself against Franz. Both were big in every way, Franz might have been harder from a more active life, and there was a dark burning violence in him, the shimmering heat from a volcano, which would give him no time to stop and think once the trigger of his passions was jerked.

Allison was surprised to find that he was not thinking of the gun, only violence from Franz's person.

Franz put the gun on the table, then went out into a store and came back with a six-volt battery in a leather case, slung like a shoulder holster.

'Your equipment's pretty complete,' Allison said.

'Haywire stuff is no good,' Franz said. 'Everything must be steady and quiet. There must be no warning.'

It was getting dark outside. Allison's taut feeling of expectancy and excitement increased with the growing of the darkness, and he began to feel edgy and impatient for Franz to set out.

'Go and see Kate,' Franz said, adjusting

the battery carrier against his powerful body. 'She'll show you the room.'

'Okay.' Allison went casually. At the top of the stairs there was a yellow glow from one of the oil lamps. As he came into its pale he saw it streaming from the girl's room through the open door. He went to it and leaned his arm against the jamb. She was lying on the bed, still in the shirt and jeans, wiggling her bare toes and watching them, almost with amusement.

'He's going soon,' Allison said, his heart beating strangely in his throat.

'Leave it a good while,' Kate said, and laughed at a sudden motion of her toes. 'He's very suspicious. He may come back to start with.'

'Why doesn't he take me with him?' Allison watched the puppet show of her toes.

'He likes to suffer,' she said, and laughed again. 'You don't know him. If there isn't a man here he thinks of men I might have had and storms and groans and hits me.'

'What!'

She turned her head and looked up into his angry face, then smiled.

'You're a very civilised person, aren't you? It's nice to be hit sometimes. But of course,' her voice took on a mocking imitation of his, 'we don't do that in the city, old boy.'

He laughed suddenly, and saw her eyes narrow in speculation.

'It was a neat probe,' he said quietly, 'but I don't happen to be in the city.'

She looked away to her toes again.

'I'll see you,' she said, as if losing interest in him.

He turned and went downstairs into the hall. Franz was standing there equipped for his expedition. Allison watched the slim, deadly little rifle and felt a cold corkscrew twist in his bowels.

'I'll be back,' Franz said, looking down as he made himself comfortable in the battery sling.

The yellow light of a rising moon shone in the big doorway. Allison lit a cigarette.

'I'll wait for you,' he said.

'I may be some hours,' Franz replied.

'I've nothing to do,' Allison said.

'Okay,' Franz said, with a shrug. 'You wait.'

He went out of the doorway and down the steps, hesitated a moment, looking at the moon, then he turned to the left and moved silently off. Allison put the cigarette in a bowl on the table and went swiftly to the door. He made no more noises than Franz had done.

He stood on the steps a moment watching Franz's shadow melt into a mass of little moon-spilt trees beyond the corner of the house, then he went down the steps and quickly along the grass edge of the gravel to the trees.

Once amongst them, the moon struck the birch trunks like tarnished silver and the shadows became confusing. He stood for a moment listening intently. He heard the faint sounds of the man moving in the wood and went quietly after them until he could see the moving shadow again, following a twisting path. Allison kept amongst the trees. Twice Franz stopped and looked back, as if suspicious of a follower, but Allison stayed still amongst the little trees and the camouflage of the moon and the leaf patterns it threw was enough in the still place.

The warmth of the day was still in the trembling air and the smells of the wood were rich in the calm night. Allison felt every touch at his senses while he stayed motionless praying for the man ahead to go on.

The little wood broke into the wider spaces of the lake forest where great oaks reached, like gnarled Atlases, supporting the sky. There was grass underfoot and the ceiling of the oak leaves made ink patches on the ground, so that moonbeams slanted through the breaks like light through a cathedral window. There was less stillness. Now and again there was the scurry of some small animal starting away from the hunter ahead, and birds suddenly beat away from branches and flew with a crackling and thrash through the higher branches. The hunter did not pause for these but went on quickly. like a man increasing his pace as he nears his objective.

Allison made his way from tree to tree, using the inky patches of the shadows, his nerves tense and quick. The ground began to slope down and then ahead there shone a strange light from the ground, silhouetting Franz's figure against it. For a moment Allison could not understand what it was, and then he saw Franz stop by the light.

'The lake,' Allison breathed. 'Of course. The moon on the lake.'

He stopped by the foot of a great oak, staring down at the man by the water's edge.

The lake, Allison thought. Surely he doesn't shoot fish?

Franz was standing there, his gun slanting towards the water, his bulky apparatus hung about him. Now he put the gun on the ground by him and looked round. Allison kept close to the trunk of the big tree. Franz unslung the lamp, and then sighted it like a camera across the lake.

The first beam of the light struck slanting on to the water some way out and pierced it, turning the silver water into a smoky burst of greenish light under the surface.

Allison heard the clatter of the reflector as the lamp flashed out on to the water. Morse, undoubtedly, but Allison's morse was back with his Scout days, more letters had faded with time, and the speed was far too great for him.

But the fact that Franz was sending morse to the surface of an empty lake was startling enough without adding the need for translating the message.

The clattering ceased after several seconds of transmission, Franz slung the lamp to him again, picked up the rifle and went away along the wild path overhanging the drop to the water.

Allison hesitated, looked back, and then turned and made his way towards the house again, going quietly and quickly, guessing as he went.

Perhaps it was some trick of bouncing the light off the water, but who was to receive the bounce and where were they? In the air? But why not shine the light directly up? — except that Franz had been under the trees there. Yet there were many breaks in the trees . . .

As he went he trod on a twig and the snap made him start and look back. He went on, and remembered sharply that there had been no sound but the clacking of the lamp in the wood. There had been no whine or roar or beat of aircraft engines, then, or before, or after. Then who could have been in the sky?

The receiver must have been on the far side of the lake somewhere. He threw memory back to his boyhood, bringing back the picture of the far side of the lake. It was different from this, quite different. On the far side the tall spikes of a pine forest had always pricked the sky, strangely, suddenly different from the forest side in which he now moved.

Then he remembered the island, the little clump of bushes and trees in the middle, and the funny mud bar that ran out to it from the pine forest side, and which you could see, like a strange strip of golden light, three feet under the water.

The island. How could he have forgotten that? The very throne of adventure. Perhaps even the crude attempts of his to build a hut of small bush branches still remained there.

He remembered the perilous first time of treading the mud bar out to the island, fearing every moment it would crumble and slide away into the bottomless lake, taking him with it.

He recalled the odd, panicky feeling then, and wondered why he had had it, when he had been able to swim at that time.

He saw the white cliff face of the house between the little birch trees, moon reflecting in the windows, making them like eyes, and the mystery of Franz receded in his mind and he saw only Kate lying on the bed watching her toes.

As he came nearer he saw the yellow light from the bedroom window had gone. He stopped and looked round, listening. In the distance an owl screeched suddenly, as if warning someone of his approach. He went on and up the steps, as silently as he had followed Franz. In the hall there was the acrid smell of his burning cigarette in the bowl, guttering in stinking paper against the bottom. The moon struck in like a solid slanting beam, cutting the darkness sharply, but his eye caught another glow from the left.

He turned and saw the door to the ruined wing standing wide. Moonlight slanted down on to the rubble beside the one-time corridor, and reflected back into the shadows against the sound wall.

He saw Kate moving along there, slowly, carefully, stepping over fallen bricks on the half-hidden carpet of the corridor. She was going carefully, looking for something in the wreckage on her right. She stopped and he saw her pale face turn to look back. For a moment he thought she could see him standing in the shadows of the hall, but she looked away again.

Suddenly he realised that she was looking for him.

She had found him there before, and when he had not come, she had gone back to the place where she had seen him hunting.

He went to the doorway. She stopped again, doubtfully now.

In the still night he heard a sound, an odd shifting sound. He looked up and saw a fine spray of mortar spill down from the broken roof above the girl. She twisted her head sharply and looked up, but from her angle she could not see what he could watch with a sick horror.

The broken line of the roof was wavering slowly. More and more pieces of debris began to spill down, and then he saw a great spilt appear in the wall behind her, widening like gigantic, distorted jaws. The whole front of the wing behind her was starting to collapse.

He ran forward suddenly, tripping on the fallen debris, ducking the new that was beginning to rain down.

'Stay there!' he shouted as she started towards him. 'Stay!'

A broken slate struck his shoulder, numbing it with pain and he ran on, almost blind now from the thickening storm of plaster dust raining down. He tried to keep the picture of the collapse in his head, judging the part that was falling now did not quite reach to where she was. The crumbling place began to roar with the thunder of an avalanche. He kept close to the wall on his left, feeling it bulge and move against him like a living body, but through the shattering smoke of the dust storm he saw her, white and isolated in the whirling mess.

He reached her and gripped her tightly to him, pressing her against the moving wall. She shouted something he could not hear in the ghastly tempest of sound. He felt the floor shifting under his feet and clutched her even tighter, in a desperate attempt to protect her. The wall tumbled against him, pushing him forward to the edge of the broken, shifting floor, as he held her like a doll in his arms. Something struck his shoulder, and a great weight pressed his back, forcing him down and down into the crashing heart of the disaster. He began to fall, twisting and stumbling on parts of a world that crumbled away from his feet. The smoke dust stifled him, blinded his eyes with grit, and all sense but that of holding her died in the awful holocaust.

They became still while the crumbling world moved and heaved around them, groaning in blackness. A heavy pressure held him across his back, but the earthquake world gradually stilled and there was a dying groan fading into an uneasy whisper as small rivulets of powdered mortar still trickled from the standing parts of the wall above them.

He felt her body beating against his in the stifling darkness.

'I can't see,' she whispered. He felt her tremble, but she stilled it by tensing her body.

'The stuff's on top of us,' he grunted. 'Got to be careful. If we move too suddenly, there may be more . . . Something — in my back. Keep still. I'll try and shift it . . .'

Slowly he began to twist his body from the hips, but the weight would not move. He relaxed a moment, then tried again. Something began to crack and scrabble like rats running away, and then suddenly the weight gave.

There was a slithering crash, something fell across his lower leg, but there was a sudden brief shaft of silver light thick with dust breaking down upon them. He twisted his neck and looked up. The moon shone strongly, and against the silver sky he saw the tottering, leering wreckage of the west roof, poised over them, caught somehow at the edge of the ruined wall fifteen feet above them. He held his breath as he saw it. Half-way up towards the saw-toothed sword of Damocles he saw the frayed edges of the floor where they had stood, timbers precariously poised over a crater in which they lay.

'We must have — gone down into the cellar,' she whispered and he could feel her breath on his cheek. 'Look! The roof!'

As they watched, the edge of the broken roof sagged and partly crumpled. Slates fell around them as they lay there, and once again he covered her with his body until the minor fall had stopped.

When he looked up again he saw the roof shifting uneasily, as if it were supported only by some eccentric pole.

'We've got to be careful,' he said, with a strange grin at his understatement. 'That lot's balancing on a hairline. If we shift anything, it'll come down on us. Just a few tons of it.'

'Can you move?' she said breathlessly.

'There's something holding me by the shoulder,' he said. 'Can you see it?'

She strained against him, straining her neck into a painful angle until she could see.

'It's a beam,' she gasped. 'Just the end of it. Don't move! It's propping something else!' She looked up at the crazy, slowly moving roof above them, then began to drag her hands up between their bodies. 'If I can get my hands out — But be careful.'

He strained his body inwards to try and release the pressure on her arms so that she could raise them higher. The beam creaked behind him as he strained, and something started to fall, with an ominous little slither and rumble. He stayed still, and so did she.

'It's stopped!' he breathed. 'Try again.'

She got her hands out and over his shoulders, pressing her cheek hard against his neck to try and see down to where the beam was.

'I've got it,' she said. 'I'll try — and lift — '

She caught her breath as she strained to lift the beam to relieve enough of the weight for him to move without disturbing it.

'Now,' he hissed, and began to ease out from under the beam, turning sideways. As he went a brick rolled away from under his arm and he stopped moving, holding his breath, and looked to it. It seemed to be lying in debris on the edge of something black a few inches from him.

'All right?' she gasped. 'It's — getting heavy.'

'Wait. Rest a second,' he said and became still as she let the full weight of the beam press down on him again.

'Okay now,' she panted, and once more strained to take some of the weight from him.

Slowly, desperately listening for any sound of shifting, he began to move slowly sideways until the beam was almost clear of his shoulder, then suddenly the ground beneath him shifted. It seemed to take on a slant and bricks and bits of rubble slid gratingly away from him to the edge of the black a few inches away from him.

Sweat got in his eyes as he lay quite still, waiting for the awful movement to stop, but he saw two bricks go over the edge of the sloping floor and tumble into the blackness.

He saw them fall, heard the clatter of them striking some sort of wall, racing away downwards under them, until their clattering became faint. He found himself subconsciously listening for a splash, the echoing sound of them striking bottom, but it did not come. The bricks went on down, down into nothing.

'It's stopped,' she breathed.

'Better hang on,' he gasped. 'Think this out again. We seem to be hanging over a well. What we're on tried to tip into it just then. Must be balancing on the edge.'

He felt her body tremble again. He could see her face upturned, almost see the reflection of the hanging roof reflected in her bright, frightened eyes. She flicked her glance towards him and steeled the fear out of them; he could feel the tenseness of the effort she made to hold her panic in check.

'We must be — on the passage floor,' she said, in a husky little voice. 'I don't remember a well — '

'Maybe it opened up in the — the earthquake,' he said. 'Don't want to rock over the edge. Lie still. We must think again.'

'Any good shouting? Franz — '

He twisted his head until he could see the awful, slowly moving roof from the corner of his eye.

'I've got a thing about the walls of Jericho,' he said.

There was a sudden little scream of wood grating on a brick or stone where something settled down towards the hall.

'I think I'll go that way — under the beam,' he said, his voice hurting in his dry and dusty throat. 'Getting further under it might lift it and put the balance on this — what we're lying on so it won't topple — that way.'

She nodded and took her arms from him.

'The only thing is — this will hurt,' he said.

She nodded again. He began to twist his body slowly, forcing it in under the beam, pressing on her right side as she lay on the wrecked floor. She saw his face shine with sweat in the moonglow until suddenly he shifted his arm with a little rushing sound so that at last he had a purchase on the floor with his elbow. Slowly, steadily, he pressed up.

'Can you — !' he gasped.

He felt her strain under him, trying to move out. He pressed harder. Sweat broke out anew as something slithered down a gritty board, and he caught a glimpse of her eyes staring wide at the tottering roof above them. Wood began to creak faintly, resisting his growing lift.

'I can — ' she panted. 'I can!'

She writhed and he felt her moving sideways beneath him. The pain in his leg was becoming like a cramp where the weight pinned it. She moved sideways, breathing fast, until suddenly the board tilted on the edge of the well.

'Stay!' he gasped.

She became still, holding her breath as if breathing might overturn the wrecked floor.

'I'll try again,' he whispered, and pressed up. Faintly the debris creaked and rustled, at any moment likely to topple and upset the hairsbreadth equilibrium of the tottering roof. He could see the end of a beam against the wall moving slightly as he raised. It was at the base of the cracked and broken wall on which the roof still balanced and as it moved he saw a crack in the brick through which the moonlight showed; it was widening as he moved. He stopped, keeping his raised position.

'Something's going to go,' he breathed.

'I'm nearly — nearly out,' she whispered.

'If you think you can get free,' he said, and coughed the dust in his throat partly clear, 'get up and run away from my head. Away. Get it!'

'It might shake — ' she hissed desperately.

'Do as I say,' he gasped. 'I know about buildings — which way they

99

fall — Ready? I'll hold it.'

She nodded and held her breath. He strained up. From the edge of his eye he could see the crack in the wall growing wider, brighter, like a grin. She struggled, and then with a wild beating of his heart he felt her dragging free, away from under him, moving bricks and rubble beyond his head. The crack grew brighter, he seemed to see a great shadow blotting out the sky above him as the great canopy of the murdered roof swung out over him.

'Run!' he shouted. 'Run!'

She scrambled free and over the piles of the rubble.

'Run, run! Keep on! Don't look back!' he cried.

She scrambled and reeled towards the end wall, got a grip on the broken top of it, and then looked back. As she did it, she saw the great roof almost planing down, like the racing, curling top of some gigantic wave and the thunder of collapse roared and seethed in her ears. The place where he had been was suddenly lost in the mighty wave of collapsing wreckage and smoke dust rose high into the silver sky. Momentarily she closed her eyes against it, the grit hurting them so that when she opened them again the settling mess was a blur of tears and shadow.

Then in her bare feet she ran, tripping and stumbling, back towards the place where he had been, now covered with an armadillo back of curving slates mixed with the brick and broken wood of the walls and floors.

She gasped on the edge of sobbing.

'Allison!' she cried. 'Allison!'

Wood creaked in uneasy settlement and that was all. She knelt down and began a futile attempt to push the mass of rubble aside, then sat back on her legs and just stared across the devastation. The dust on her face was streaked with tear streams. She drew a deep breath, then bit her lips and grabbed up a piece of broken planking. With that she started to dig a way down to where he had been, gasping and breathing little words of despair as she worked.

4

The brilliant beam of the lamp struck through the shadows from the hall door and fell upon her, stained and bedraggled, desperate with hurt. She looked up into the full glare without feeling its intensity.

'Franz!' she cried, breathlessly. 'Franz. Here, quickly!'

He came without hurrying, clambering over the new piles of wreckage, almost as if testing each foothold before he used it.

'Quickly!' she pleaded.

He came to her and she stood up, her bosom rising and falling with the extremity of despair.

'He's under there — Allison,' she gasped.

Franz looked at her, white and streaked in the moonlight, then he looked round.

'What happened?' he grunted.

'More fell,' she said. 'He saved

me — but he — He's under there!
Quick, Franz!'

He grabbed her arm and held it tightly
as with the cold strength of a vice. She
drew in her breath with a hiss, and then
stayed still, staring at him.

'What was he doing here?' Franz said.

He felt her shiver as he held her.

'I thought he was here,' she said in a
burst. 'I came and he saw me from the
hall. It started to fall. He came and got
me. He laid on top of me. He saved my
life, Franz. He saved me. If he hadn't
come — I'd have run the wrong way.
And he — he got me out — '

A cold swamp of fear flooded her soul
as she saw his dark, brooding face.

'If he wasn't here, where was he?'
Franz said.

'He must have been — in the hall. I
don't know. All I know is he came after
me when the wall started to fall. Franz,
we've got to get him out.'

He began to pull her towards him. She
resisted, but his strength was too great.
He turned as she stumbled, slipping on
the rubble, being pulled his way.

'Franz!'

'It's the best that could have happened,' Franz said between his teeth. 'Surely you can see that?'

'But you can't leave him! I told you — '

'He's probably dead,' Franz said. 'If he is — good.'

'Oh no, Franz!' She began to sob. 'No, no!'

He turned on her as if he would hit her.

'You wouldn't cry for him, would you?'

'But Franz — '

He smacked her hard across the face. She swung her head to one side to avoid another blow and became quite still, held by his fierce grip on her arm.

'He doesn't matter,' Franz said. 'It's a bit of luck for us, that's all.' He became motionless, listening. There was no sound but that of her stifled little sobs, almost a whimpering.

'If you cry for him, I'll kill you, Kate,' he said, grabbing her shoulder and shaking her bodily.

She relaxed and put a hand to her forehead.

'I'm all right,' she said in a panting little voice. 'It's the shock. I thought I was going to die. And he — '

'He's dead,' Franz said. 'There's no sound of him. It's luck. Come on.'

He dragged her at first, then she went with him, growing steadier as she went.

'Perhaps you're right, Franz,' she said.

They clambered up the sloping pile of debris to the hallway door. Franz bent at the top and picked up his lamp. She hesitated while he watched her.

'Go on,' he said gruffly.

She went up and through the door into the hall, where she stopped and slowly rubbed her forearm where his grip had hurt her. Upon the long table she saw the gleam of the rifle barrel where Franz had put it. She snatched it up and swung it round to him, moonlight gleaming on the barrel as it pointed to his heart. He came on, and suddenly she let it fall and put it back on the table. His face was terrible to see then, and he stopped as if anger held him paralysed.

'Why do you try to frighten me?' he said savagely.

'I don't know,' she said, turning her back on him. 'I just wanted you to feel frightened as I did — out there.'

'There are no cartridges in it,' he said.

She shrugged, and suppressed a thrill of fear as she sensed him close behind her.

'You must forget him,' Franz said.

'It's difficult, staying in this house and knowing — ' She let her shudder go this time.

'One can forget,' Franz said. 'And it won't be for long now.'

'But if he is alive — '

'He can't be alive,' Franz said. 'There must be tons of that stuff fallen now. Don't think of it like that.'

He put his hands on her shoulders.

'Don't,' she said, shaking them off. 'I'm so all-to-bits I could scream.'

She walked away into the kitchen, and he followed closely behind her, watchful, suspicious. She went to the brandy bottle and held it up against the bright moon.

'This might help,' she said, bitterly. 'It isn't so easy to forget, Franz, when you saw it happen.'

'Yes,' he said, slowly. 'Sleep. That is it. Let's drink a toast. To luck! Good Lady Luck! It isn't often one wants to thank her.'

'No,' she said, and picked up two glasses with the fingers of her hand. 'Not often. Come, then, Franz. Let's drink it. We might see her in dreams.'

She went out into the hall. He followed again, watching her every movement as it was outlined by the soft blue of the moonlight. They went up into the bedroom where Allison had kissed her and a sudden great sickness ran through her, but she went round the bed to the far side of it and sat down, putting the bottle and glasses on the table there.

Franz came and lent on the other side, watching her. Tiredness weighed him, and the strain of watching her increased his weariness. He had not slept for many nights, and the bottle, as she raised it, seemed to offer something more precious than anything else.

'Sometimes it doesn't work,' he said, and sat on the bed and shook his head.

'We'll have enough to make sure,' she said, and poured a generous measure into a glass. She handed it to him, then poured some for herself.

He held his, with his eyes on her as she turned and lifted her legs on to the bed. She saw him watching and raised the glass.

'Skoll,' she said. 'Lady Luck!'

She drank, and after a moment, so did he. He put his glass on the floor, then rolled on to the bed beside her. It was warm, and he felt his feet like lead in his shoes, but he was too tired to do anything about it.

There was a mirror on a dressing table angled so that, lying on her side, she could see him beyond her, lying flat on his back, staring at the ceiling. She could see the restless fingers of his right hand feeling the shape of the little pistol in his belt pocket. She kept her eyes on the mirror, steeling herself against the effects of the doped drink. So far there was nothing to feel but the lingering taste of the poor brandy. She lay still, staring into the mirror, listening to his slow breathing.

Every few seconds a great force of black fear for Allison gripped her heart and squeezed it free of emotion, and she became frozen again waiting for the sleeping draught to start its poisonous lethargy.

Suppose it worked before his?

The very thought of that made violent reaction in her push back the slowly creeping sleep in her brain.

Franz's breathing grew slower, deeper. She strained to look into the mirror, trying to see if his eyes were shut, but the more she tried to penetrate the cheating moonlight, the more grew the encroaching shadows round the edges of her sight.

The draught was beginning to work. She clenched her fists until they hurt and held her breath, as if the tautness of her lungs would stop the gathering shadows of the drug.

His breathing seemed to be regular and deep now, but she could not be sure. The drug was beginning to paint fantastic impressions in her brain, twisting sight and sense, making dream scenes of reality. The mirror seemed to be receding from her, as if it would vanish like a ghost through the wall. She lifted herself on one elbow as if to will it to stop disappearing. The veils of sleep were growing thicker, like whirling smoke in her brain, gradually suffocating, so that feelings became numb, then solid, then dead. Fear for Allison now became a black, heavy thing, too heavy, too powerful to be worth the fighting.

A panic arose through the gathering darkness in her and she put a hand to her bosom to feel her heart still beating.

She dare not wait much longer. The stuff was smothering her; the coils of sleep were winding round her like a shroud.

She turned and looked at him. His eyes were closed, his chest rising and falling slowly, his hand clenched the shape of the little gun in his pocket.

Seeing him, the strain seemed to die in the wish to sleep, and she almost fell back to the bed again. Then slowly she began to get off the bed, dragging her legs, trying not to wake him but being clumsy and uncertain with the creeping hold of the drug. She left the bed and swayed back against the wall. For a moment she feared he heard her bump against the panelling, and stood there, shaking her head, as if that would clear it.

He went on breathing slowly.

She went unsteadily round the bed towards the door. He turned and groaned, disturbed subconsciously by the movement. She stopped by the door, trying to keep her eyes from closing, knowing only dully that danger was there.

He settled again, and she turned and reeled out of the door, trying to keep one thing in her mind, to stay conscious until she got down to the kitchen.

Going down the stairs seemed like floating down some well with black walls of smoke. She stumbled and swayed against the banisters, clutching them desperately, as if by her grasp she could haul herself up out of the sea of stupor that held her.

At the bottom she held the newel post for a moment before she let go and went slowly through into the hall. Upstairs, Franz groaned again, as if uneasily feeling that his companion had gone. She did not hear it. Nothing mattered any more but the kitchen.

She fumbled as if the dream was on already. She sloshed water into a cup, split it as she upended a tin of salt into it. The salt stream shivered and shook over the floor and her wrist. The mixture was ready at last. She dropped the tin on the floor and it rolled over against her foot, then she drank the emetic.

It was the desperate intent, the will to defeat the drug that won the battle after several minutes. What remained in her stomach was cleared, but what was in her blood was fought down by sheer refusal to give in.

Still partly dazed, she went back into the devastated wing. It stood bright and ghastly in the moonlight as she picked a dangerous way over the heaps of rubble to the spot where he had been. She stopped near it.

Some of the wreckage had shifted and tipped down into the well, for part of the mouth of it now showed black amidst the debris, but the part of the roof still stood there, like some nightmare tortoise, slates shining in the glow.

She stopped still, holding her breath, a strange sense of unreality still lingering from the draught, but straining to listen.

From somewhere beneath the wreckage she could hear movements, scratching, scrabbling. She knelt down by the edge of the fallen roof.

'Allison! Allison!'

From deep down there came the murmur of an answer, but too muffled to be understood. Desperately she looked around her. The hump of the fallen roof seemed like a little mountain, and her first despairing instinct to get some sort of tool and dig died. She had not the strength, and even had she, there would be no time before Franz came to. The draught would not last forever, strong though she now knew it was.

She bent right down and put her face to a gap between fallen beams.

113

'Can you hear me?'

Again a mumble, far down in the mess. As she got to her feet a great swelling gratitude filled her breast that he was alive. She did not stop to analyse the feeling, but began clambering away over the rubble to the back of the house where the stables were, her heart beating wildly with excitement, her head, though not clear, working in bright little clicks, one of which settled on the Landrover.

It was standing where Franz had left it by the stables, a coil of wire rope propped in front of the radiator. It was for pulling trees, but Franz had used it only once to pull over part of the wall which had been dangerous. Now she got in, started up and drove to the edge of the wrecked wing.

She got out, unhooked the wire and fixed one end round the bumper. Then she clambered over the rubble uncoiling the hawser as she went. As she came to the mass of the fallen roof she had too much slack. She turned and looked at the truck, then climbed on over the roof slates until she found a part of the

114

structure, then she fixed the wire round a beam and scrambled back, stumbling and slipping on the tumbled muck. Once in the seat of the truck she started up again and with the engine ticking over began to back, slowly as a worm until the wire grew taut. She stopped, her eyes on the tumbled mass of the roof, and then began to take the strain, moving back an inch at a time for fear the whole broken mass would break up altogether. The roof began to move, but the slates were crushing up, gaps between them growing bigger. Slowly the little truck went back and gradually the fallen mass was pulled aside, beams began to shift and fall, bricks tumbled, dust rose again in little explosions, white in the moonlight. She stopped, got out and climbed back into the devastation to where she knew he was. As she drew near she saw bricks fall aside and two hands thrust up through the mess. She uttered a little exclamation, and almost fell in her hurry to be there. She knelt down, and began lifting away the broken timbers until she saw his face, black and stained.

'You!' he gasped and coughed with the dust in his throat.

'Are you all right?' she gasped, working hard to clear the stuff.

'All right?' he said, shoving bricks off him. 'Pinned down like a dead man and me claustrophobic!'

It took fifteen minutes before he climbed painfully out and crouched on one knee, taking great, slow breaths to still some pain in his chest.

'There's blood on your shoulder,' she said, and pulled his shirt aside. The wound looked black in the moonlight. 'Come inside with me. But please — don't make any noise. He thinks you're dead. He made me leave you there.'

He got up heavily and limped weakly over the rubble until suddenly he stopped.

'Come on!' she whispered.

'No,' he said breathlessly. Horror shone in his eyes. 'Look there. Have you seen him before?'

She looked to where he pointed and caught her breath sharply as she saw what it was. A man's body, half buried, the upper part now uncovered by the

116

shifting of the wreckage, lay amid a cradle of broken bricks, white face and hands upturned to the moon as if in some kind of prayer.

Kate stood quite still, staring at the dead man. Allison swayed slightly from dizziness and shock, a hand on his wounded shoulder. She looked round at him and gave a little grimace.

'Sit down a minute,' she said.

He sat down heavily on a piece of broken wall and let his head fall forward, as if he would faint. She watched him for a moment, then scrambled away over the rubble to the end of the hawser. She unhooked it from the broken roof, then began to coil it on her arm as she made her way back to the Landrover. She went quickly, and at the end jammed the wire coil back behind the bumper and got into the driving seat. She backed the little truck away and swung it round back to where Franz had left it. She switched off and ran back to Allison, breathing fast.

'You're feeling bad,' she said.

He lifted his head and drew a long, grating breath.

'If I hadn't been face down, I should have — ' He shook his head and got up unsteadily, his eyes on the dead man unbelieving.

She took his arm and guided him back towards the rear end of the house and into the kitchen. Once there she stayed still, listening to the beating of her heart, trying to hear if Franz was moving. The house was silent.

Allison slumped in a chair. She pulled his shirt off his shoulder.

'It's not too bad,' she said, as she washed it.

'I hurt all over my damn back,' he grunted.

She left him a moment, went to a cupboard and brought out a Scotch bottle.

'There's nothing in this but the stuff,' she said, with a wry grin. She poured him some and he drank it gratefully. 'Now listen . . . Franz mustn't know you're still alive.'

He felt her hand tremble on his bare flesh.

'He thinks I'm dead?'

She nodded. 'And he means you to stay dead.'

He felt better for the whisky, much clearer in the head, the choking effects of claustrophobia wearing thin.

'Who is that man out there?' He caught her wrist and held it, looking into her face. 'Do *you* know?'

'It's a man who came,' she said, suddenly breathless. 'I though he went away again. I didn't know — '

His eyes still on her face, he let her go.

'There's a bullet hole in his head,' he said, and winced.

'I saw,' she said, and let a bandage unroll from her hand then stopped suddenly to listen, holding her breath.

'It was something outside,' he said quietly. 'Some animal.'

She let her breath go, and began to bind the wound.

'You've got to go,' she said in a whisper.

He shook his head. 'No,' he said. 'Not now. If I went and Franz found out, what would happen to you?'

She turned her face away from him.

'He wouldn't find out,' she said.

He caught her by the waist as she went to move away and stood up, holding her.

'Do you want me to go?'

She stood motionless for a moment, then gasped in a deep breath, spun round and pressed herself against him.

'No. No, I don't want you to go,' she said breathlessly. 'But you can't stay here. He'll kill you. He nearly killed you then. It doesn't matter, you see. You don't understand, but it doesn't matter if he kills you. You saw that man — ' She stopped a moment. 'It could be you. If you stay, it will be.'

'I'm staying,' he said, holding her tightly.

'You can't challenge him,' she whispered.

'I don't want to. I'm going to stay because I want you.'

She hugged him tightly for a moment, then laughed a little.

'It isn't worth the risk,' she said softly.

'I'm the only one who can weigh that,' he said. 'I'm staying around. Somewhere close. Very close.'

He kissed her and her response was electric. He felt the thrill of her through every muscle in his body. She drew her head back and looked at him.

'I don't believe you ever would have jumped in the lake,' she said, shaking her head slowly.

'I never meant to,' he said. 'You had it wrong. It was just now you saved me — not this morning.'

'Quits,' she said, and suddenly pushed him away. She stood back from him, legs apart, put her hands on her hips. 'Nobody owes anything, so you go.'

He pulled his shirt back over the bandaged shoulder.

'You feel groggy still?' she said, watching.

'I'm a mass of pain — till you kiss me,' he said. He grinned but she saw he was leaning heavily against the side of the table. She turned her head again, fearing a sound from above. She listened intently but he did not share her alarm; he was too much in pain to fear Franz's coming then.

'I thought I heard him,' she whispered,

staring back at him.

He turned and picked up the Scotch bottle.

'Do you mind?' he said, and poured some more into his glass. 'I think it's shock. They say it has odd effects. Though I think it might be exhaustion from prolonged panic. I really thought I was buried alive.' He drank, then let his glass down as he saw her watching him, her teeth clenched as if some terror held her.

'I was feeling it, too,' she said huskily, and turned away. 'You can't stay here,' she went on, after a while. 'You can't face him like that, and if he finds you — '

'I won't let him find me,' Allison said, 'unless you want me. But I'll be here.'

'Where can you go that he won't find — '

She flicked her head round.

'Kate!' The sound of Franz's voice was distant, but clear.

Allison stood quite still, a grin on his face.

'He's coming!' she whispered.

'I'll be here,' Allison breathed, and went by her to the partly open door of the room where Franz had fetched the lamp battery.

'No, don't — no!' she began, then turned towards the hall door.

The shuffling of Franz's quick, uneasy steps was coming nearer. Kate put her hands to her hair, stayed still a moment then called called:

'Franz? What is it?'

Franz appeared in the doorway, untidy and lowering, his darkness accentuated by the moonlight.

'What are you doing?' he demanded.

'I woke up,' she said. 'That stuff made me thirsty.'

Franz picked up the Scotch bottle.

'Funny drink for a thirst,' he said darkly.

'Not with a head like mine,' she said coolly.

He looked around the room.

'How is it that you get a bad head — not me?' he said, turning back to her. He came closer, staring suspiciously.

'You forget — I was in that fall,' she said quickly.

He stopped.

'I'd forgotten,' he said. 'I thought it was only — him.' He ran a hand over his face. 'That stuff makes you muzzy. It's not much good. Only a short sleep.'

He passed her and went to the sink to draw water. She watched him apprehensively as he tipped his head back, drinking. It seemed an exaggerated attitude, typical of his strength and power. When he had done he wiped his mouth on his forearm and turned round to face her again.

'I wondered where you'd gone,' he said hoarsely. 'Thought you might have heard something.'

His brow was low, shadowing his eyes from the moon. He took her arm.

'Let's see everything's all right,' he said, turning her to the hall door.

She hesitated a moment, then let him guide her into the hall to the still open door to the ruined wing. She held her breath as they came near it.

'Anything wrong?' he said, stopping.

'No.'

'Not scared?'

'I'm all right,' she said angrily.

They came to the doorway and looked through over the great mounds of wreckage.

'Quiet as the grave,' Franz said, in a kind of awed voice. His hold on her arm tightened and she stiffened with the pain of it and glanced at his heavy face. He was staring, eyes narrowed across the rubble range. She looked in the direction of his stare. Both looked at the same thing. He did not speak.

'It's a man,' she said quickly.

'Yeah.' He breathed the word, still staring.

'Hadn't you better look?' she cried.

He stayed a moment more without moving, then reached out past her, caught the edge of the door and slammed it shut.

'Nasty,' he said. He let her go, brought a handkerchief from his pocket and wiped his face and the back of his neck.

'It was the man who came here,' she

said, half accusing, half sickened.

'Yeah,' he said again, and jerked his head back towards the kitchen. They went back into it and he took the Scotch bottle and drank from it, his eyes on her all the time. 'The new fall must have shifted some stuff.'

'What are you going to do?'

He grinned and showed his broad white teeth.

'Shift it back again,' he said. He went to the stove, lifted a lid and pushed a coffee pot on to the hotplate.

'What's going to happen if someone comes?' she said in a husky little voice.

'You mean strangers? Why should they dig about?' He turned to her and leaned back against the range bar. 'Why should anybody come?'

'Because of the man, Allison,' she said, slowly. 'He was on the run. There must be somebody behind.'

'He'd lost them,' Franz said, staring curiously. 'He wasn't scared once he got here. He knows what a good place a haunted house is. People pretend they don't believe in them, but they never come near, just the same.'

She went to him and pulled a cigarette packet from his trouser pocket. She did not speak until she had lit one.

'How much longer have we got to stay?' she asked.

'Not long,' he said.

'Every hour makes it more dangerous,' she said. 'And there could be somebody behind Allison. It's all very well for you to say he's not afraid. He could be. You couldn't guess people's feelings. You can't be sure on what they'll do next.'

'Allison's dead,' Franz said between his teeth. 'Nobody follows dead men.'

'Nobody knows but us that he's dead,' she said, and felt a shiver run through her.

His dark eyes were sharp.

'Cold?' he said ironically. 'Or do you think Allison might haunt the house?'

'Don't be a fool.'

He came close behind her and almost whispered in her ear.

'You're sure he was under that fall?'

He put his hands on her shoulders

and felt the sudden contraction of her muscles.

'Yes. When I got out there was another fall. It trapped him. You saw there was nothing of him when you got there.'

'I saw,' he said.

He let her go and turned away. She glanced round as he did and saw a faint smile begin on his face.

'Why are they so long coming?' she said, suppressing a shudder.

'Don't be impatient,' he said. 'It may not be so pleasant when they come.'

'It can't be worse than waiting.'

He leaned against the sink and watched her carefully.

'You are trying to think of something,' Franz said. 'What?'

'I'm upset,' she said.

'You've got to be hard. You know that,' he said, cocking his head and watching her. 'I think it's good he is dead. I don't like your upsets.'

He leaned away from the sink and turned towards the door where Allison hid. She gave no sign of alarm, though he seemed to her to be watching for some.

128

At the door he hesitated and turned back to her.

'You can't leave me,' he said. It was a warning, a threat.

She stiffened, her eyes bright.

'I can go any time,' she said slowly, bitterly.

He went close to her.

'You can't go from me,' he repeated.

The scornful smile came back to her face, but her eyes were very bright as she watched him. He grabbed her wrist; his automatic threats, a combination of hurting and making himself feel he was holding her.

'You stay,' he said.

Allison saw the first blow, and for a moment stood rigid. At the second, he drew back from the door gap and stood against the wall, a mass of pain and indecision. He could not face the black, angry man like this. The courage in him wilted, yet he kept his eyes on the gap.

'You won't keep me like that!' Kate cried out and struggled violently to break the cruel grip on her arm. She kicked at his legs and he stumbled with her against the wall, but did not let go.

He struck her again across the face with a flat hand, and then suddenly, she ceased to struggle.

'All right,' she moaned. 'Leave me alone.'

Allison covered his face with his hands and tried to make the torment of his cowardice die down. He could not hear sounds from the kitchen for the thudding of his own heart.

I could not face him like this, he thought; I'm broken down. I can't move fast enough. I can't —

His thought jerked round in him and he knew the truth.

The excuse was sound, for pain racked him then, but pain had not been the reason. The reason was that he feared Franz, feared to face him, feared to challenge him.

'You shall come with me again,' Franz said, menacingly.

'Where?'

'Outside. I want to make sure about Allison. He is important.' His voice grew soft, purring, as if in this move he knew he would frighten her more than by any other.

'You don't believe me, do you!' she cried out. 'But he is there! How could he have got out? No one could move all that — '

'It is just to make sure,' Franz insisted quietly. 'You know that we can't take risks. We have to be close together these last few days. There must be absolute trust, absolute certainty. If there should come one little break-away between us, the whole affair might collapse, and then you know what would happen, don't you, Kate? You and me — we would be dead. It would be foolish not to do anything that would save our own lives.'

Suddenly Allison dropped his hands from his head and looked towards the gap. He took a step as he saw Franz push the girl towards the hall door, and for a moment burnt with the crazy idea of rushing out and taking the man.

But he stopped as his foot dragged on the stone floor and made a shiffing sound. He stood quite still as he saw Franz stop and look slowly round, holding the girl close to him.

'What was that?' Franz said slowly.

Inch by inch Allison retreated from the line of the doorway as if Franz could see through into the darkness of the little store room.

'Nothing,' Kate said. 'It was my shoe.' She scraped her soft shoe on the flags of the floor. There was a faint likeness to the first sound. Franz stayed a moment, unconvinced.

'Come on — if you must!' Kate said desperately.

'Okay,' Franz said.

They went out of the kitchen. Allison was alone in the silence.

Franz felt her resisting as they crossed the hall again. By the open door she stopped.

'What's the matter?' Franz said very softly.

'It's dangerous down there,' she said in a little gasp.

'It's dangerous up here,' he bantered. 'It's always dangerous for us. Why be scared now?'

'I'm scared of death.'

'You're scared,' he said, his grip tightening on her arm. 'But I think it's me you're scared of . . . Something has happened to you today, my little precious. It's this man Allison. You can't keep a secret like that from me. It's very foolish to try. One sees it in your face, in your body, and because of that I know he is not dead. If he were, you would be crying, you would be broken — but you are not. You are merely frightened of me — frightened that I shall find him!'

'It isn't, Franz,' she said, trying to keep her voice from trembling.

'Where is he?'

'Under that!' She pointed through to the wreckage.

'Where is he?' Franz repeated.

She turned abruptly, ignoring the sudden searing pain in her arm as it twisted and clawed at his eyes. She did not succeed but she hurt him and he staggered back a pace, letting go his grip on her arm. As she broke free he put his hand over his eyes a moment, then blinked and started forward to her. She snatched up the little rifle by the barrel and raised it like a club above her shoulder.

'I'll hit you!' she cried. 'If you don't leave me alone, I'll hit you!'

He stopped still, looking at her, his big hands crooked like claws.

'I told you,' he said hoarsely, 'if there's anything like a little breakaway between us — '

They stood there facing each other, motionless with the strain that tensed the very air around them. Franz knew that he was near death then, and his whole being was alert, quivering on the brink of action, ready for the slightest sign of weakness in her hating eyes.

'One breakaway,' he repeated very softly. 'One is enough to kill us both. You stand no chance alone, Kate. You stand no chance with Allison.'

She did not move but stood, still threatening him with the club, and then a great shudder took her. She let the gun fall in her hands, and then dropped it altogether. She turned her back on him.

He went up close behind her.

'We must not fight, you and I,' he said.

He turned and then, as if certain of her defeat, went back into the kitchen.

5

Allison stood in the moonlit yard, bewildered, his head humming with pain. He put his hands to it to stop the shrieking of the ache, which seemed to be growing worse. The dreadful feeling of being smothered again was gathering round him like a black pressure in the air. He saw the stables and went unsteadily towards them, cursing his weakness. He reached the doors and reeled against them and stayed leaning there for several seconds before he recovered enough to open them. He went through into the path of the moon shaft from the opening, pulled wide the car door and fell lengthwise along the seat. The pain and suffocation merged, gathering thickly about him, and he was sinking into a blackness which had the soft welcome of death itself.

He became quite still but for the slow, pained breathing. Outside Franz's slow footfalls shiffed on the grit-covered cobbles of the yard, but Allison did not hear them.

Franz lit a cigarette, looked all round him, then shook his head and went back to the house.

★ ★ ★

The engines were roaring with the strain of trying to lift the machine, but the power was not enough. He was flying in amongst great oaks, under the silver threads of power cables cast about in the high air. To touch any one of these obstructions would be to fall helplessly to the ground below. He steered carefully, tension making his hands tremble as he threaded a perilous way under the great laughing wires and in the maze of the great poles and trees. He opened the throttles wider and wider, but the plane would not climb out of the hazards. He made a sudden turn to avoid the great mass of an oak ahead of him, and felt the machine begin to stall. It juddered desperately and then began to spin down, flat as a saucer, slowly, sickeningly, so that he wanted to fall faster.

'You're not to swim there,' his mother said. 'It goes right down to the middle of the earth.'

'No, mother,' he said. 'There's treasure in the house, and a big lady in velvet and she cuddles me to her chest so tight I can't breathe. I want to get away but she laughs.'

'You will be safe by the house,' his mother said. 'But you must not go in or someone will take it from us.'

And suddenly he saw his mother wore velvet and she cuddled him against her big bosom and made a purring sound.

'It's a pretend treasure,' she said softly. 'You must not go in the house.'

'I saw it,' he said. 'It was all gold and big jewels like the king's. It's behind the painting of the Spanish lady and the pirates.'

'If you touch it, they will take it away,' his mother said.

He was eating bread and jam and the taste was sick in his mouth. It was like eating wet sawdust but he went on eating it.

'The police will come and get you,' his mother said, but she looked like the Spanish lady.

'If I go in the house, they won't,' he said.

'Why have you come back,' the Spanish lady said.

'I came back for Jim,' he said.

'I am not rich,' she said. 'And the pirate is watching.'

'It is Franz,' he said. 'I know him . . .'

The sudden fear of Franz rushed through him rising like a peak through the dream and he awoke suddenly. watching the dashboard dials winking in the moonlight. He lay still, trying to find where he was.

It is Franz, he thought, puzzled; Franz the pirate in the picture buying the Spanish lady on the Caribbean quay —

But was it?

He sat up abruptly and strained to recapture the detail of the picture in his memory. It had hung in the long dining-room, where now only the chairs were standing. He had always gone there last because he had been in love with the Spanish lady. She had stood so proud, so beautiful, so scornful of the leering pirate who had ripped her dress from one shoulder down to her waist. He had always rescued her so many times from that awful, fearless, leering face —

Franz?

He closed his eyes willing himself back through the years, could even feel the fine black knob of the carver as he leaned on it, staring at the picture, enraptured . . .

Had it looked like Franz, or was it imagination distorting memory by a present fear?

And yet —

He opened his eyes. His head was clear, and the pains had become more a stiffness. He got out of the car and stood up. He put a hand to the wound Kate had bandaged and went to the doorway. Everything was still beneath the brilliant moon. He went slowly along towards the ruins of the wing where the picture had been. Near the place where the dining-room had been he stopped.

The dead man had stopped praying to the moon. He had gone altogether.

Allison stayed quite still, listening, as if someone might be near, watching him. He moved on again over the rubble to where the lurching top rail and knobs of the old carver chair still stood proud of the desolation.

The body had lain by that. The picture had once hung behind it. This must have been the great black chair he had leant against to watch the lovely colour of his heroine all those years ago.

He stood on a mound of brick, trying to see where the line of the partition wall had run, then turned and looked to where the man had lain.

In front of the chair, hands out to the wall. As if he had been facing the wall when the place had collapsed about him, trapping him.

He had been facing the picture — if the picture had still been there. Facing the picture at the very moment of the collapse — the explosion.

He squatted on his heels, a hand to his shoulder, easing the aching pulse of

141

the wound, and looked carefully over the small area of the wreckage where he knew the man had been.

There was part of a big skylight lying broken and twisted behind the chair, and he remembered that there had been one over the centre of the big room, so there had been no floor above, just the roof.

The rubble here would not be so heavy as on the other parts where the upper floors and then the slate roof had come down on top. That was why the chair still showed.

He went forward and began to measure with his eye the approximate half-way mark along the partition wall, where he remembered the picture had hung.

It was piled with broken wood and strips of lead from the gutters with jagged pieces of broken plaster scattered everywhere.

He looked towards the main part of the house, listened a moment, then began to lift aside some of the debris, carefully and slowly. He worked for twenty minutes before his fingers scrabbled aside a mass of crumbled plaster and muck and revealed the dull gold edge of a frame.

The find seemed like a triumph, and he began to clear the rest of the frame quickly, until he saw that the picture faced upwards. The boards of the back were not uppermost but showed in the frame space.

He found a thin edge of canvas close to the frame itself.

The picture had been cut out.

An emptiness held him, as if the great single purpose of a life's journey had faded like a mirage. He felt the thudding of his pains begin again, and he stood up and held his shoulder, looking from the edge of the frame to the chair where the man had been.

There was nothing now to show anything at all of what could have happened there, unless a few dozen tons of debris were cleared away.

How had the picture gone just when he had recognised the pirate? A thing fled out of his search at the very moment that he seemed to have seen its meaning. It had the very elusiveness of a dream, the awful frustration was the same.

He looked to where the dead man had been by the lurching chair. He had failed too, his hands outstretched to the picture, still groping in death.

Where was he?

Franz must have taken him away.

He stood quite still looking over the small area where the picture had been, only his eyes moving. Then suddenly he heard a sound from the house; a voice raised in an angry word.

He turned and climbed away over the rubble, going quickly but trying to be careful. He came in amongst the reaching hands of the little trees, half crushed under the fallen bricks, and stopped and turned back. The shivering leaves covered him and as he crouched there waiting, they became still, a dappled stencil against the moon.

Franz came at the hall doorway, his body pale against the black shadow. Slowly, carefully, he began to come along the remains of the corridor floor, where the front wall now was a jagged rampart only a foot or two high.

He stopped. Allison looked back to the doorway and saw Kate there. She was standing quite still, watching Franz.

'He's gone,' Franz said, and then his voice grew louder, sharper. 'He's *gone*!'

Allison was too far away to see any reaction from the girl, but Franz's attitude suddenly struck a chill word of fear right through him. It was not fear of Franz any more, but the sudden terror of something he could no longer understand.

'Somebody shifted him!' Franz said.

'He must be there,' Kate said, desperation in her voice. 'By the chair. Look again. The stuff's shifted again perhaps. Look again.'

Franz moved further along the wrecked floor, his eyes on the spot where the dead man had lain, and stopped again.

'No,' he said, his voice like gravel in his throat. 'He has gone.'

'There is no one that could have — ' She broke off.

Shrill alarm ran through Allison's body.

'It was Allison!' Franz shouted. 'You lied! You lied!'

'It was not Allison,' Kate replied with an icy sharpness. 'How could he? Why? *Why*?'

Franz's voice became suddenly pleading.

'There is no one but us three!' he said. 'No one but us!'

Allison remained motionless. The fear and bewilderment that made Franz protest held him in a freezing grip.

'Perhaps it has shifted — perhaps there is a well!' Kate cried. 'Look! *Look!*'

Franz stepped off the broken floor and clumped and slipped over the rubble until he could put his hand on the knob of the great chair and steady himself.

'There is nothing,' he said huskily. 'There is nothing. He has been taken away!'

He stood there staring about him slowly. Allison almost felt the slow scan pass over the screen of trees that hid him, almost felt the gaze hesitate, sensing the man hiding there.

Franz twisted his head back towards the girl.

'It's Allison!' he said. 'It must be Allison!'

The near panic in his voice was clear to hear in the still night. For Franz it had to be Allison, otherwise it had to be — what?

There was no one else in that place; no one moving, being seen, making sounds, being heard. There was no one else in that place but the three.

Franz in his despair seemed to forget that Allison was supposed to have been buried in the new collapse. The thought that Allison was alive and free was better for him than the sudden knowledge that an unknown was working unseen and unheard in the silence.

Allison knew his feeling, shared it. He found himself crouching tensely in the little trees, listening, trying to magnify even the murmur of the earth breathing.

Franz turned and clambered back towards the hanging door of the hall where the girl stood.

'He is alive, isn't he?' he demanded.

'I don't know,' she said. 'You wouldn't let me go.'

Franz turned and looked back across the wreckage.

147

'It must be Allison,' he muttered angrily.

'Why did you leave the man there?' she said sharply.

'Until tonight I did not know he was there,' Franz said. 'Do you really think I would have left a dead body lying out there?'

'You thought that he had gone the day he came?'

'You know I did!' Franz almost shouted. 'I thought he had laid a time bomb. I told you — that was how I guessed the wing blew up. You know that! Of course I did not know he was there. Why should he blow himself up? He was no lunatic!'

'You did nothing when you saw him tonight.'

'I had to look after you,' Franz said bitterly. 'Because you wanted Allison. The dead man did not seem so important then. I could have dealt with him later on. I had to look to you. Then when I felt you were calm, I came back — but he was gone. It is Allison. It must be. You lied. He was not under that fall. He was not there at all, was he? Was he?'

'Yes, he was there,' she said. 'I told you!'

'But you tell so many lies about him. You are always trying to hide him from me. You could have lied about him then to let him get away. That's what you did, and he took the man, hid him somewhere. That's the truth, isn't it?'

'He didn't move the man,' she said. 'It's no use kidding yourself.'

'There is no one else,' he hissed.

'There must be,' she answered.

'But I would have seen — some sign — some track. I watch the paths and the track out there. I know every print there — ' He broke off, gasped in breath suddenly.

'There is somebody else here,' Kate said slowly. 'There must be!'

'But there are no tracks!'

'There must be — somewhere.' She sounded urgent, quick with fear.

'Where? Where?' he said bewildered.

'Perhaps you have missed them. There must be marks somewhere. Somebody took that body. Someone did.'

Franz turned and began to plod slowly back across the humped rubble, searching.

'You cannot see anything in this,' he said, halting. 'It is useless to look!'

She came a little way after him, then suddenly he went on towards the ruin of the old back wall. Beyond that there was the cement-dusty surface of the cobbled yard.

'If they carried him away it must show here — somewhere here!' he said.

The scuff and turn of many prints, tyre and shoe all mixed together, were there as he pointed to them, but along the line of the wall itself there were no new tracks.

Allison watched, holding his breath for long periods in case the sound of his breathing should carry in the stillness. Franz was too near. The girl came clambering over the piles of rubble and stopped near Franz, her hands on her belt.

'There's nothing here,' Franz said. 'If someone carried him there would be marks, deep marks, scuffs. Look. You see there are none.'

'Then it couldn't have been Allison, either,' she said.

He turned sharply and looked at her. 'No,' he said.

For a moment he stood watching her queerly, then he swung away abruptly and began to follow the broken, muck-strewn edges of the old walls. He forced his way by the clawing fingers of the little trees where Allison hid, and went on, his eyes on the ground.

Allison waited, trying to remember where he had trod, or if he had trod there at all. Surely he had jumped into cover when he had heard them?

But Franz was not looking for tracks away from the wall. He was looking for those close to, for tracks left by someone carrying a heavy burden, whose steps would therefore be heavy and short. He passed by the hiding place, leaving the branches trembling in his wake. He vanished from Allison's peering view behind rubble heaps as he continued his uneasy circuit of the broken walls.

Kate stood on a heap of brick, looking quickly about her. Allison would have made a sign, but stayed for fear his movement made the branches rustle enough for Franz's tensed ears to catch the sound.

She stood there, watching and listening. Faint in the night Allison heard the soft pad of the searching man returning. He appeared in a break in the wreckage by the side wall.

'There's nothing.'

His voice was dead with a strange kind of despair.

'He must have been carried away,' Kate said.

'There's nothing,' Franz repeated.

Allison saw the girl catch her breath and stand rigid, as if fighting down some emotion. A queer coldness crept over him. The atmosphere of a dream was returning; the feeling that reality slipped away when he tried to touch it.

The dead man had gone, but there was no one to take him but three people. The dead man had been carried away, but no one had left any mark.

'Perhaps — into the house?' Kate said, stiff with uneasiness.

'We were there,' Franz answered. 'No one could have gone that way. No one at all!' His mouth twisted as he added: 'Carrying a body. We must have heard it! Even if we had not been there to see, we must have heard!'

He began to scramble back over the mounds towards the hall door as if still not certain. He climbed up on to the sagging edge of the passage floor and stood there, looking down.

'Yours and mine — Allison's,' he said. 'Nothing else. You can see. It is all clear. The white dust. You cannot mistake it.'

Slowly she began to go back to him. As Allison watched he had the feeling that she was going back to him as a comforter in some terrible dilemma.

As they went into the house, Allison relaxed against the trunk of the little tree at his back. Idiotic words beat in his brain in a mad repetition.

The dead man was taken away — by nobody.

There were no signs of anyone there, but the man had gone.

He remembered the well, where the

bricks had fallen and stood up, parting the little branches ahead of him. He stared over the wreck, but between the chair and the place where the well was lay twenty feet, and half way along that distance there were the stumpy remains of the partition wall. No shock, no slide of debris could have pushed the body over that barrier.

He must have been lifted from that spot, no matter which way he had gone.

And there had been no one to lift him.

Again Allison parted the branches and stared carefully out over the rubble. There were hiding places, but Franz had already looked over that place too carefully.

There was only the well, but the bricks had never reached the bottom of it.

Suddenly the idea came to him that perhaps it was not a well, but a crack, a hole reaching down beyond the range of sound into the earth's bowels. It was an idea that brought a sudden cold shiver and for a moment shifted the danger of his position from something he could understand to something he could not.

The effect was brief. He began to back away through the little trees and the bushes until he came near the end wall of the stone stables. The moon was sinking now and the green flush of the sun faded the sky in the east beyond the pine forest.

The pain in his shoulder dragged like lead, making his whole body tired. He stood for a while against the stable wall, wondering what he was to do. His weariness and pain were turning into a kind of hopelessness, like the empty feeling that had brought him to this place.

Why did he stay? Why did he want to know about these people? He liked the girl; he wanted her, but the man was jealous. The man would kill him. What had Franz to fear in this lonely place? Had there not been one man dead already?

Jim . . .

Get out of it, he thought, his mind sheering off from the oddity of the vanished man. Get out of it. You have lost everything else, but you have your body, your life still. It is the only thing you have, but why throw it away? What is there to stay for?

They had gone into the house. He had only to open the doors, drive the car out and away. What was the chance of the rifleman hitting him before he was clear? He could hit the car, but could he stop it?

It was worth the risk.

He wanted to know what the secret of this place was; he would always want to know. He wanted the girl; he would always want her if he went now. But he had no strength left to fight them. He was not hard like Franz. He could not fight Franz.

He went along the sagging doors of the stables until he came to the pair that hid the car. They were partly open, lurching to the ground.

He looked towards the house across the thirty yards of cobbled ground, but nothing moved there. In the distance he could hear birds singing, awakening to the lightening of the sky.

He grasped the first door, lifted it from the ground and pulled it slowly back. He looked back at the house again, then went to the second door. As he moved it, the hinges groaned loudly. He stood, a chill sweat sweeping him, and again looked back to the house. Nothing moved.

He moved the door wide enough to clear the car, turning it slowly so that the hinge noise became a muffled groan. He stopped, and without looking back again, he went to the car and got in. He reached for the switch before he shut the car door and then stopped still.

There was no key.

The slow spread of sweat began again as he sat there, his fingers crooked as if they had got hold of the key, his whole body motionless until he relaxed and let his head go forward and rest on the rim of the wheel.

Then he heard the man's soft shoes grate on some loose rubble on the house step.

He straightened and turned his head. Franz was coming out of the house, the

157

silver line of his rifle slanting under his arm.

Allison slid out of the seat and backed slowly into the shadows of the stalls. Franz was looking directly at the open doors as if he knew they had been moved. He stayed a moment, then came slowly across the cobbles, his gun held low and ready.

As he backed away, Allison saw Franz hesitate and look round to the wrecked wing before he came on more quickly, and very quietly.

Allison looked behind him. In the gloom he could see the half walls of the stall divisions and beyond a wooden ladder running up through a hole in the ceiling. Haywisps hung down raggedly from the opening. He remembered it all from years ago. Once he had pretended to be a king in hiding up there, watching the roundheads searching the straw bales below.

Franz came close to the doors and stopped again. The low, slanting moon threw his shadow against one door, distorted and skewed. Allison could see

158

the shadow of his head move quickly, looking back towards the ruins again.

Allison turned, gripped the ladder and began to go swiftly up. The rungs creaked as he went. Franz stepped swiftly into the stables behind the car, gun ready and peered round through the shadows. Allison reached the top and slithered into the rustling hay.

'Allison!'

Franz's voice was soft as it called, hardly more than a whisper.

Allison became still, peering down through the opening from behind the ragged wisps of the hay.

Franz looked about him, came into the stables past the car and stopped again, cocking his head to listen. His whole frame was alert, quick, ready in an instant to wake at the slightest sound.

Then slowly, he seemed to relax, as if deciding the rustling had been the moving of a rat.

Allison's heart stopped beating with hope, but too soon. Franz looked about him again, then touched the open car door, swinging it, as if wondering why it was open. He put the rifle on the seat and turned back to stare at the ladder, his hand on his belt. He came slowly down the gulley between the stalls, looking from side to side into the shadowy places.

Allison moved slightly, withdrawing.

Franz moved on towards the ladder and as he came, a solitary wisp of hay, spinning like a sycamore seed, drifted down in front of his eyes.

Instantly, he looked up to the opening. For a moment Allison felt that the two men were actually looking at each other in the gloom. He did not move; nor did Franz. Allison could see his dark shadow foreshortened, the pale of his face upturned, his right hand on his belt.

'Allison!' Franz said quietly.

The very beams seemed to creak in the tense silence as the voice died away.

Below him, Allison saw Franz turn and looked back towards the car.

He began to go back towards it, soft footed, silent, still wondering as he searched. Allison watched tensely. Franz stopped again and came back towards the ladder. Once more he stopped and looked up at the ladder hole in the ceiling.

'Allison,' he called softly.

He turned and looked around him, then took a hayfork from hooks on the wall. He balanced it in his hands, then suddenly stabbed upwards through the hole at the hay piling at the edge of the ceiling boards.

The prongs sheered through the edge of the wood, raising long splinters and momentarily arresting the drive of the fork. Allison started back on his knees, and for an instant, Franz saw him. The fork clattered to the floor as Allison started right back through the knee-high straw into the deeper shadows of the loft.

Franz came up through the opening quickly and tumbled to one side amid the hay, covering himself against a sudden attack then lying still, peering through the darkness.

'Allison,' he said again.

He began to scramble forward through the hay and suddenly the gleam of his little pistol showed in his hand. He turned slightly, and Allison realised Franz could not see him. In that moment he jumped and threw himself on the man's back. Franz disappeared under the hay and Allison felt the sudden tension of his body muscles uncoil and strive like steel springs in an effort to throw off the assailant.

Allison strained to keep him down, smothering in the hay, but Franz was too strong and he was rocked on the man's wild back and then suddenly toppled sideways into the hay, still struggling to keep his hold on Franz.

It was as he fell that he saw the bright flash of the little gun lying on the haystrewn floorboards. He let go of Franz and as the man twisted, he snatched up the gun and crouched in the hay fingers fumbling to reach the trigger.

'Hold it!' he panted.

Franz became still, breathing hard, and did not speak until his breath grew steadier.

'I haven't come to fight you,' he said angrily.

Allison got to his knees the gun

pointing at Franz.

'We want you, back in the house,' Franz went on, sullenly.

His look was intense, so much so that Allison found himself surprised by belief.

'Me?' He stared. 'This is a sudden change! What's happened to you?'

'Come back to the house,' Franz said.

Allison laughed.

'Who goes down the ladder first?' he said contemptuously.

Franz shrugged.

'Whichever you choose,' he said gruffly.

The answer puzzled Allison still more, increased his suspicion.

'What has happened?' he asked.

Franz watched him.

'Someone else has come here,' Franz said.

'But you have seen no one?'

'I know they are here.'

'Where? The whole damned place is empty but for us!'

'There is someone,' Franz said doggedly.

'Because that body disappeared?' Allison said.

'Yes.'

'The whole place shifted. There were two separate falls,' Allison said aggressively. 'It could have been shifted with those collapses.'

Franz shook his head.

'There is someone here,' he said.

Allison leant back against the rough wooden wall, watching Franz in the growing light from below.

'I heard you talking with Kate,' he said. 'You know there is no sign of anybody but us three.'

'There is a sign.' Franz said. 'The dead man has gone.'

'So you're scared,' Allison said.

'We have to look after ourselves.'

'You wanted to leave me dead.'

Franz looked at the hay as he knelt in it.

'I hate you because of her,' he said, without looking up. 'But if there is someone here, then — ' he shrugged again, ' — better the devil you know.'

'There's a trick in this,' Allison said. 'You came after me with a gun just now.'

'I had to expect you to fight.'

'You have the answers, don't you?'

Franz muttered something impatiently.

'Will you come back?' he demanded, almost in a shout.

'If you want me back with her there, you must be scared worse than I'm thinking,' Allison said, with a slight sneer.

'I want you back,' Franz said.

Allison sat still.

'I just want to get out of here,' he said. 'That's why I came — to get the car.'

'You can't go,' Franz said.

'I must go some time,' Allison said, his eyes narrowing.

'Not now,' Franz said.

The two words seemed like the voice of fate, not Franz's at all. Once again Allison felt pain and weariness coming over him, making the struggle seem hopeless, even worthless. He fought it back.

'All right,' he said. 'I'll come back. You wait while I get down that ladder.'

Franz showed no sign of emotion either way, but remained squatting in the straw while Allison began to go down the ladder. He waited till Allison called from below.

'Okay, Franz!'

Then he went obediently. They met at the bottom of the ladder. Franz ignored the little pistol in Allison's hand. They went together out into the brightening day. There was a smell of coffee coming from the house which made Allison feel sick with emptiness. He stopped and leaned heavily against the stable wall, and as dizziness struck him he let the pistol fall. Franz picked it up, put it in his trousers pocket and kept his hand on it. He watched Allison with dark eyes.

'Go on — shoot!' Allison shouted suddenly. 'What the hell are you waiting for?'

Franz put his forearm across Allison's throat, pinning him against the stable wall, almost breaking his windpipe.

'Is there anyone following you?' Franz said.

Allison struggled to push him aside. Franz punched him in the wind. Allison went slack against the wall, choking, broken by the blow.

166

'No,' he whispered.

Franz stood back.

'There is somebody here,' he said again.

Allison sat down on a mounting stone and held his head in his hands. Franz raised a foot and kicked his hands aside. Allison jerked his head up.

'There is somebody here!' Franz said again.

'There's you, me and the girl!' Allison said.

'Somebody else now,' Franz said, between his teeth. 'Did somebody follow you?'

'Nobody would follow me,' Allison said. 'It wasn't that kind of a run.'

'Do you know who could be here?'

Allison just shook his head as if the question did not interest him.

'Have you seen anyone?' Franz persisted.

'Nobody,' Allison said with bitterness. 'If I had I'd have gone with them, don't worry. There was a dead man over there. Why should you care who took him? It may save you hanging!'

Franz grinned mirthlessly.

167

'I didn't kill that man,' he said.

Allison leant back against the stable wall, his head turned up to the dark man.

'What does it matter if somebody's here?' he said huskily. 'Sooner or later somebody'll come and find what you're up to. Why not now? What's so strange about it that you get scared till your eyes turn yellow?'

'If they came in the open — yes!' Franz said, showing his teeth again. 'But they don't. They are silent, secret. You do not see them. You do not hear — '

'What does it matter, the man has gone?' Allison broke in, his eyes narrowing. 'It it just the *way* it was done that scares you? Or is there something about the man that scares you? If so, why didn't you hide him yourself? Why did you leave him in a place where more falls could show him up to anybody to stare at?'

'I didn't know he was still there.' Franz said. 'I thought he had gone, days ago.'

'He was caught there when the place blew up,' Allison said.

168

'Blew up?' Franz said sharply.

'Blew up!' cried Allison. 'What else could have wrecked the place like that but an explosion?'

'There was no — '

'It was blown up!' Allison shouted. 'And I'll tell you more about it. It wasn't a bomb. That wouldn't be big enough. It was something worse, like gas blowing up. It blew up from inside as if every damned room in the place was filled with gas and the fire ran through it and it became one ghastly expansion that burst the place apart. That's what it was, Franz, and you know it was. But *what* gas was it? There isn't any ordinary gas here. What sort of gas gathered in that house till it burst at the seams, Franz?'

Franz's jaws were taut.

'I do not know what caused it!' he snapped. 'It happened when I was in the wood.'

'And what did you do?' Allison said. 'Did you tell anybody? Did you call anybody? Did you bring the police or the fire brigade to see if it was safe? Did you do anything, you caretaker? No,

169

you stayed here with Kate, shrugged your shoulders and sat around, still waiting. Half the house blew up, but that wasn't enough to shift you. You had to go on waiting. Waiting. What for, Franz?'

'We are paid to wait,' Franz said. 'That is what caretakers — '

'You can cut out the caretakers,' Allison said. 'You may have pretended to be that at the start.'

'The people will not pay to rebuild!' Franz said angrily. 'When the people say, 'Leave it — let it fall' what is there more for us to do?'

'Then why stay?'

Allison got up suddenly.

'Why stay?' he repeated. 'Why sit waiting, keeping strangers away — for that's all you're suppose to be doing. That's why Kate went for me with a gun when I came. That's why she wasn't sure and doped me while she went to find out who I was. Well, she didn't find out, Franz. Nor will you. I brought nothing with me that can help you at all. But you were both scared to frighten me away as you might have done anybody else. You were scared because you thought I was being followed, and you had to find out. Why? What does it matter to you if ten thousand men suddenly come into this park after me? What can they see, Franz, but a house with a wrecked wing? What else is there to see? . . . '

He went closer to Franz.

'There's nothing to see, Franz,' he said. 'There's nothing to see but a fallen wing. It might puzzle them, but that's all. What else is there to see?

'There's nothing at all, Franz. It isn't what's here to see. It's what's *going to be here* to be seen that scares you. It's what's *going to* happen that you've got to keep from curious eyes.

'What is going to happen? What is going to happen, Franz.'

The girl appeared suddenly and without making any noise that they heard.

'There's somebody moving — in there,' she said breathlessly. 'Under the floor in the corridor.'

'There's a cellar down there,' Allison said impatiently. 'That's no mystery — '

'The cellar was blocked in by the

171

fall,' Franz said quickly, and turned towards the house. He hesitated there a moment, then crossed the cobbles in his soft shoes.

'He's on edge,' she said, looking at Allison. 'It's you. He keeps thinking about you all the time.'

He took her wrist suddenly. Suspicious she looked up at him, then her eyes hardened to diamonds as she saw his expression.

'Do what I say, and don't call him,' he said in a quiet, tense voice.

'What — '

She began to struggle. He turned the wrist behind her and as it began to hurt, pushed her forward, away from the house towards the trees bordering the lake. She gave a little gasp. He went close behind her and put his hand over her mouth.

'Don't try!' he hissed. 'I'll hurt you!'

She struggled again but stopped when the pain shot through her arm. By then he was thrusting her forwards into the wood. He took his hand from her mouth.

'You're crazy!' she gasped. 'You can't — '

'Get on!' he said roughly, and pushed

her forward amongst the trees.

'He'll kill you!' she panted.

'I'm used to that idea,' he said.

Twice he looked back before the screen of the trees cut them off. Franz was still in the house; the stable yard was empty.

'When I was a boy I knew all this place,' he said, as he pushed her onwards. 'There's a cave. I'll show it to you. I used to think I was hiding there with the beautiful princess I'd rescued from the dragon. I didn't think I'd ever be sitting there with the dragon!'

She kicked back at his legs suddenly and made a twisting effort to escape. His grip tightened on her and she became momentarily rigid with the pain, then relaxed and went on.

'You've got to let go — some time,' she gasped.

'I'll be ready then,' he promised.

He realised that she had not shouted because she was frightened of what Franz would do. He had got his hand bitten for nothing.

They went on through the trees until

the water, sparkling with the new sunlight, flashed upwards on to the arching roof of the leaves. He came to the base of a great tree, sprawling like Titan on the grass. It was still there, the hidden entrance to the little cave amongst the roots.

He forced her down towards it.

'If you try anything, it's going to hurt,' he said.

She bent and entered the cave, and because of the awkwardness and an instinctive wish not to hurt he let her wrist slack in his grip.

In a flash she tore herself free, turned and went for him as he came head first into the cave. He caught her, but she was fighting like a cat. He tripped and went down into the sandy earth, hanging on to her while she hit and bit him in a wild fury that almost got her free. When he knew he could not hold her writhing body any more, he tried to throw himself sideways and managed it, pinning her to the ground underneath him. He caught one wrist, then another and at last held them both to the earth. They became still for a moment, panting

174

to get breath back.

'Better say you won't try that again,' he said.

'Let go my arms. You hurt!' Her eyes blazed but there was no sign of surrender there.

'Better say,' he repeated.

She made a sudden twist that took him completely by surprise and he toppled to one side. She snatched her wrists free and twisted round as she lay getting into a position where she could have sprung up in the direction of the entrance. But he caught her just before she could make the leap. She scratched and hit his face, but he held her through all the wild violence of the moment, until at last she stayed still in his arms, panting for breath.

There was a moment of stillness, a tension that broke suddenly. She grabbed him round the neck and kissed him with a wild passion that flowed into him from the contact with her. The cave, the world of danger dissolved around him and there was only the girl and unreasoning passion burning them.

6

There was only the sound of birds outside the cave. They crouched there together, staring at the multicoloured sparkle on the faintly ruffled lake.

'He must come,' Allison said, frowning. 'You know he must!'

'Something has gone wrong,' she said, her eyes gleaming with the reflection off the water. 'Something has happened. I know.'

'He would have come here, wouldn't he?' Allison said, turning to her.

'If he thought you had gone — yes.' She nodded.

'Whatever he's guarding is in the lake or under it,' Allison said.

She took her man's shirt from the floor and struggled into it.

'We must go back,' she said urgently. 'I know something must have happened. I know.'

He held her arm.

'I can't just go back like that,' he said. 'It could be part of a trick. He might be waiting deliberately, guessing where I am.'

'No, no!' she said. 'No, something must have happened. I know it because he would come here at once. He would have to. You don't understand, but he would have to if he thought you were trying to find out — '

He saw alarm and fear in her light eyes, and he could see that there was no falseness in them. She was frightened for Franz. He felt a sudden burst of jealousy.

'We'll carry on waiting. In case,' he said.

'But listen I tell you I know — '

'Then you can spend the time telling me why.'

She shook her head slowly, watching him.

'I don't know everything,' she said huskily. 'That's the truth. I don't.'

'You must know why you're here?' he said angrily.

'To get away,' she whispered.

'What do you mean?' he said, startled. 'Get away where?'

'Out of the country,' she said. 'That's why I came. That's why I'm waiting. Franz promised me.'

'You want to be smuggled out?' he said, amazed.

'Yes. That is why I am waiting. But if anything happens to Franz, it is no use waiting any more. Don't you understand? He's the only one that can do it for me?'

'But why is he here?'

'I don't know what he is doing here,' she said. 'All I know is he promised he would get me away, and I am waiting for that.'

He sat back on his heels, watching her.

'I can't believe it,' he said.

'It's the truth,' she said.

'What's your reason for going?'

She stared out over the sparkling water, not seeming to feel his hand on her arm.

'What's your reason?' he repeated, shaking her arm.

178

She looked at him coolly.

'Murder,' she said. 'I killed somebody.'

He let go of her.

'I asked Franz if he would get me away,' she said. 'He said he would but I would have to take a risk and wait several days, and I would have to help him see nobody came here.'

She spoke slowly, sulkily, even, staring at the lake.

'Franz was here already?' he asked.

She nodded.

'How did you find him?' he went on.

She did not seem to hear. He repeated the question.

'We should go back,' she said, with sudden violence. 'I know something has happened.'

She sprang to her feet and ducked out of the cave into the tree-split sunlight. He went after her, following an instant of surprise. She ran fast on her long legs through the wood, but he gained on her, and she knew it. Suddenly she ran to the left, stopped by a tree and turned facing him with her back against the bark. Her bosom rose and fell deeply, and her eyes were bright and strangely flecked as she looked at him.

'Let me go back,' she panted, in a strange pleading little voice. 'Please let me go back!'

He watched her, suspicious still.

'All right,' he said. 'We go back.'

She let her head fall to her chest and for a moment stood relaxed. Then she straightened and nodded to him. They walked away through the wood, back towards the house. His eyes searched every shadow as they went, constantly expecting Franz, but they saw no one. Nor did they speak, for he listened for every sound that might not have been a bird or a sudden scurrying animal in the undergrowth. Now and again he stopped, and a few impatient paces ahead, so did she, looking back at him, as if some invisible chain held her back to him. When he had looked round, he went on again.

'You are used to it,' she said, in a puzzled voice.

He looked at her.

'I remember a lot,' he said. 'Specially here.'

'It was such a long time ago you were here,' she whispered.

'It doesn't seem like it.'

They came in sight of the corner of the house. It stood silent in the morning sunlight. From a parapet a starling cocked its head at them and a swallow suddenly flashed out from beneath the eaves and swooped away towards the ruins. Nothing else moved.

Suddenly she went forward, unable to hold still any longer. He followed. Neither made a sound as they kept to the grass-grown edges of the cobbled yard.

Near the back door of the house he went ahead of her and stepped in. There was no sound of any movement in the place. She came up close behind him.

'Something's happened!' she whispered. 'I told you!'

He went through into the hall, listened at the foot of the stairs, stared out of the front door. As he watched there the birds seemed to be flying away from the house down towards the wood. A cloud passed over the sun and for a moment the house was in shadow, and he felt almost the touch of a chill breath in the hot air.

He turned and looked at her standing quite still, her face white, tense.

'Was it down here you heard something?' he said.

'Under this,' she said. 'But the cellar's blocked in.'

'Sound can travel,' he said.

He looked along the great corridor, a sense of oddness and danger increasing as he saw something wrong there, but could not recognise it.

From above there came a sudden scuttering sound. He turned quickly and looked at her again, then he started up the stairs, going quickly and quietly. She followed him into the landing-room above. The sound seemed to come from along the corridor where the bedroom was. They went down it, looking into the rooms, but saw nothing moving.

Then the noise came again from one of the rooms they had passed. He turned back, passed her and began to run. He darted in at the door, then stopped. A big bird was sitting on the window sill by the pane that was shut. It took off, flew up the shut glass with a fluttering of wings, then landed again without seeing the freedom in the open leaf next to it.

'It's a damnfool bird,' he said, breathlessly. 'I must be getting nervous.' He laughed shortly.

'Where could he have gone?' she said, as they went downstairs again.

'He could have left the house.'

'Not while he was looking for something — or somebody.'

'Well, he isn't here, is he?' he cried angrily. 'I don't see him or his corpse — ' He saw her expression, stopped abruptly and turned on his way down the stairs.

Once in the hall again he began to walk slowly down the long corridor, staring to right and left, trying to get another angle on what he was seeing. She came alongside him.

'Can you see anything?' she whispered, sensing his strain.

183

He stopped and looked back along the passage.

'Something is wrong here,' he said. 'I don't remember ever seeing it like this before, but I can't place it . . . Is it the sun? Yes, I think it must be the sun — This is the time of day I often came, and I used to know every inch of the place, and I'm trying to remember . . . '

He went slowly and then stopped.

'It's this room,' he said, stopping and pointing. 'The big room — two doors but there's no light in the doorway . . . '

He went slowly into the room. It was big. Smaller rooms led out of it, and the furniture was covered in dust sheets, just as he had seen it years before. He stopped and heard her breathing close behind him.

'Why do you keep thinking back to those days?' she said. 'What makes you?'

He turned to her.

'Naturally I remember. I spent a boyhood here.'

She shook her head.

'No — it must be something *now*,'

she said, watching him. 'What made you come here? When did you think of coming here?'

'In the middle of the night before last,' he said. 'I was worried. I was getting to the end of my tether. You know how it can happen. Suddenly you can't fight any more and you want to run back through the years to a place where there wasn't any trouble — '

'The wing blew up that night,' she said.

'The night before last?' he said, starting.

She nodded.

'And that's when the man was killed in there?' he demanded.

'I don't know,' she admitted. 'I'm not sure of that. There should have been nobody here but Franz and — '

'You?'

'What's happened to him?' she said, quick fear showing in her eyes.

'He could have gone out of here,' Allison said slowly. 'He could have done anything.'

'He wouldn't have gone,' she said. 'For

one thing it's too close to the time, and for another he wouldn't leave me with you. He'd try — '

'How do you know about the time?' he broke in.

'From the way he was behaving,' she said. 'He was screwed up these last few hours. It wasn't you. He was angry and jealous about you. This was something twisting inside him, making him expect something. I've got to know him these last few days.'

He moved into one of the adjoining rooms and slowly carried out a search of the whole undamaged part of the house. The entrance that had led to the cellars was blocked by fallen brick and wood that nothing short of a bulldozer could have moved.

'Where could he be, then?' he said, wiping sweat from his face with the tattered remnants of his shirt.

They were back in the room from which they had started. It was so big it killed the sound of his voice.

'Someone must be here,' she said.

'You heard something moving, he went

to look and vanished,' Allison said, with faint irony. 'That proves nothing. It could have been something he chased.'

He looked towards the slatted shutters over the windows.

'I never saw them drawn before,' he said. 'That's what cuts the light into the passage . . . Why did he do that? . . . Do you know, this room is like the one where the picture was. The reflection. I never realised that before.'

He leaned against a big table and shook his head.

'I'm so tired, I can't think,' he said. 'But if you say the time was near, why shouldn't he have gone? He was meant to go, wasn't he?'

'He would not go and leave me.'

'You're too damn sure,' he said, bitterly. 'Let's get coffee, or something. I'm shot.'

'Come with me,' she said.

He shrugged and followed. She did not go into the kitchen but to the door overlooking the wreck. A bird flew off a timber peak, and that was all.

'How in hell can you think anyone's

here in this silence?' he protested. 'There's nobody in ten miles!'

'Then where's Franz?' She rounded on him sharply.

'You worry — ' He turned away from her, irritated and abrupt, and then saw the little pistol lying in the corner of the hall. It was the proof that she was right. Franz had come into the house with that little gun, and he would not have let it go willingly.

She did not speak, but followed the direction of his glance and saw the gun.

'I knew,' she whispered. 'Somebody took that body. Now they've taken Franz. There's us two left. You don't think they'll let us go, do you?'

'Who in hell's 'they' — if they're not Franz's pals?' he cried. 'What is this? Some secret battle? Where are they fighting? Where are they?'

He crossed the room and picked up the gun. He unclipped the magazine and saw it was still loaded.

'He didn't fire at anything,' he said, and slipped the gun into his pocket as he looked round him.

He had the feeling now that something was there, something was hiding in the bright sunlight, watching him from behind. It was incredible, it was mad, but it was there.

At last he looked back at her. She seemed calm, satisfied now that she knew he shared her fear.

'I was right,' she said in a little voice.

'Guess so,' he said. 'There must be something.'

He stared out at the ruined wing, frowning.

'He said there were no marks of anybody near,' he went on. 'He'd have known. Well, how else do they come? There's nothing in the air. We should have heard any machine up there. No. There's just one place I've seen here.'

'That well?' she said.

He nodded. They went out on to the rubble, treading carefully, watching every shadow cast by the sun, as if the hidden enemy could be a lizard hiding in a crack, or a rat perched on a overhanging lip of broken timber. Allison held the little gun in his hand.

The birds had gone from the house, and sang away in the distant trees. The air was hot and still, so still Allison was tempted to look sharply round him when his own foot sent a little cascade of dust and muck slipping down a crack.

As they came nearer to the well where he had been buried, the choking sensation of claustrophobia smothered him again. He stood still, the sweat freezing on his skin.

'What's the matter?' she whispered from behind him.

He fought the smothering feeling down and cleared his throat.

'Felt queer,' he said, and went on again to where the black mouth of the well showed amongst the wreckage.

The walls, which they could see in the sunlight for a depth of a few feet were of stone, smoothly round and glistening with damp.

From somewhere there came a faint sound of water trickling, but it seemed a great distance off.

Allison picked up a brick and tossed it down into the black pit. They waited for the splash, but there was none. Instead there was a faint rushing sound, then silence.

'We want the lamp,' he said.

'I'll go — ' she began but he caught her arm.

'Not alone,' he said. 'Let's look around first. I can't see any marks that somebody crawled out of here. There'd be some on the edge — '

He looked round to where the tilted chairback stood, and the dead man had been.

'There were two cellars,' he said slowly. 'One main storage place under the hall somewhere, and a wine cellar almost under the dining-room — there!'

He pointed to the chair, then slowly made his way back across the wreckage to the broken edge of the corridor floor. It was like the edge of a railway station platform at that point with darkness underneath for a short distance. He bent to see under it, leaning on a slanting pile of timber. She came close behind it.

'Suppose — somebody's down there?' she whispered.

'That'll be better than being stalked by a lot of ghosts!' he hissed. 'It's giving me bad nerves. I'd sooner see somebody.'

He moved into the darkness, bending low, and then stopped.

'Here's the door,' he said. 'Still in the frame. I think I can open it — No. It's unfastened. Keep behind me.'

His voice was very soft in the silence. As he pulled the door open, it creaked slightly. There was some kind of light glow in the cellar but he could not see where it came from. He stepped down into the greyness, she holding on to his arm. There was scattered rubble on the cement floor, but otherwise the cellar seemed intact.

'Nobody here,' he said.

Wine racks stood about, a still for a barrel, packing cases.

There was a slithering sound behind them, then a crash as the door slammed shut, and a rumbling that lasted for several seconds.

Allison ran to the door, grabbed the handle and pushed hard. it did not move.

'Was it somebody — ?' she cried in alarm.

He stood back from the door.

'Somebody — or another fall,' he panted, turning round. 'We'll have to see if there's another way out. I don't remember.'

It took two minutes to explore every crack in the walls and to find that there was no other way but the door.

'Perhaps something like this happened to Franz,' she said, in a breathless voice. 'Trapped — '

'He would have yelled,' Allison said in a colourless tone, and sat down heavily on a crate. 'He would have made a row.' His voice grew angry. 'We should have heard him!' He let his head fall heavily into his hands for a moment.

She dropped on to her knees in front of him, her hands clasped between her breasts, her eyes shining in the gloom.

'He can't be dead?' she whispered. 'He can't be dead!'

He lifted his head and stared at her, anger increasing as he saw the line of tears in her eyes.

'Why can't he? What does it matter? You said he was just someone you met — someone who was going to do you a favour. You said that, didn't you?'

He grabbed her shoulders and shook her. She did not resist but the tears came faster and spilled on her cheeks.

'Forget him!' he cried. 'What does he mean, anyhow? He was just someone who was waiting. That's all he was. Now it's our turn to wait. What's the difference? What does he matter? You made love to me, didn't you?'

Her face hardened, and she shook her head.

'You don't understand,' she said. 'I shared the waiting with Franz. I shared the danger. We always knew this might happen. That's why we had to watch. When you've been through that with somebody it makes him a part of your life. Without him, I might not have had much left.'

'You love him?' He shouted at her.

She shook her head. 'It isn't like that. We shared and it was dangerous. That's all.'

He sat down on the box, looking at the grey shadowy ceiling, trying to control his turbulent feelings; trying not to think of Franz, and what had happened to him.

'Who did you kill?' he said.

'A man. I shot him — several times.'

He looked down at her.

'You'd hang for that,' he said, and felt a savage kind of delight in feeling that she could be hurt.

'I know,' she said. 'Franz saved me.'

He got up. She sat back on her heels as if he had pushed her. He went round the walls again, into the angles of the odd-shaped place, searching for a crack that might widen, but his search was of little value for inside him his soul burnt with fierce jealousy. He tried to understand the passion, why it should have arisen in so short a time, but there was no explanation. It had happened.

When he came back she was still kneeling there, staring at the crate he had sat on.

'Who was he frightened might come before his friends did?' he said. 'Not police. Nor anyone like them. If he said

195

he would get you away, it must have been smuggling of some kind. That's all that fits. Then who are the others? Who are the ones here now?'

'Enemies,' she said, in a very low voice. 'That was all he ever said. He didn't talk about them. He didn't want to think about them. He just hoped his friends would get here first, then it wouldn't matter.'

He went away again and leant against the wall, trying not to feel jealousy.

'He was signalling to something in the lake,' he said, as if repeating something to himself. 'Something under it, could it have been? A sub? How would it get there? A river?' His eyes brightened and he turned back to look down at her. 'Under the house here? A forgotten river?'

She looked askance at him, but clearly had never heard of such a thing. He came and sat down on the crate again.

'Do you know, that's about the only thing that could explain all this?' he said. 'Just think a minute. The bottomless lake, we always called it. Say that it's just very deep. And suppose there was a tunnel of water running from somewhere down it, out into the sea bed somewhere. If you had a little submarine you could navigate right through here, bring in what you wanted. Take away what you wanted. Why, it's so very simple, Kate!'

He reached out and took her shoulders, the excitement of discovery making his anger less.

'You saw the picture of the pirate, Kate? It was exactly like Franz.'

'I saw it,' she said, in a mechanical sort of way. 'I said about the likeness.'

'What did he say?'

'He just shook his shoulders and said everybody had a double somewhere in the world,' she said.

'You mean he hadn't noticed it?'

'I think if you suddenly see a picture of yourself it does not strike you at once. You can only see yourself in a mirror, and that's the wrong way round. You know that.'

'Then what?'

She shrugged and looked sullenly at the floor.

'After that it wasn't there. That's all.'
He let her go and sat back.

'I say it was his father,' he said.
'Someone very close. Someone who came
here and posed for the artist who used
to live here. And while he was here,
he found out about the river . . . Say
it was twenty-five years ago. Before the
second war. Franz is what? Austrian?
German? A tunnel like that could have
been a valuable property to a German
going back to his own land just before
the war.'

'The war was long ago,' she said.

'But wars still go on,' he said. 'Wars
of ideas, of plans and opposing plans,
wars of politics where millions can be
made in a night before the chessboard
changes again. That's the thing, Kate.
There's big money in that kind of war.
All you need is to get information out
of one country and into another. But
the radio and the phone and the rest
are all monitored. And also you have to
trust people bought from the other side,
and when the prize is money, you can't
be too sure of your buy.

'But if you can bring in your own man, or keep a regular information service of men, you could do very, very well. You let loose somebody else's secret, there's a sudden fear, a fall in the market of that country. Only slight, perhaps, but once there's a depression, it rises up again, sometimes above par. You can play it like a fish, if you know the game and if you're organising the wires that make the fish rise.'

'How do you know this,' she asked, sharply, her eyes narrowing.

'It was my business, messing around with money,' he said, and smiled as if at something far in the distant past. 'Only it didn't roll my way.'

'You said you were a country boy.'

He looked at the door, then round the dim walls of the room again.

'Somehow there's a way up from that river into this house,' he said. 'It must be. It is the only reason the house could have been kept empty. Keeping empty houses is expensive, specially where you have daily caretakers, too. But the job of the caretaker is to dust and wipe away marks

199

of dust, so that neither he nor anybody else who ever came would see if the place was being used occasionally or not. It is the only thing that can explain it all — a gateway to the world that Franz's father found, twenty-five years ago. And Franz was here. I wonder why?'

He laughed shortly.

'Why are you so silent?' he said.

'I'm trying to think how we shall get out,' she said, watching him.

'It is by trying to think things out that you might find a way,' he said, slowly. 'For instance, if there is a way down to a secret river, it must come up in one of these two cellars.'

'There is the well, also!' she said.

'I think the well has been covered for years,' he said. 'The bricks didn't splash because they were caught by bushes, or some kind of vegetation growing down there. The explosion blew the well cover off. That's what must have happened. You see, the well was under the house, but there was no cellar there, so it must have been built over years ago.'

'Well, if you think that the way out is

here somewhere for God's sake try and find it!' she cried suddenly. 'You've got to find him. You've got to find Franz!'

He sat there, staring, even the aching of his body stilled. He stared at her with hatred burning in his eyes, then he got up and walked slowly away to the blocked door. He looked at it. She watched his back, and the light of fear came into her eyes, as if she sensed his rising fury and she was scared of it at last.

'Franz is dead,' Allison said, picking the wood of the door with his fingers, as if trying to tear it. 'He was right. There is someone here besides the three of us — two of us now. Someone who has been trying to kill us. When you went to search the ruin last night, the roof began to fall. Once we were trapped, more fell. A man came here and the place blew up. Franz has gone.' He turned back and looked at her, grinning at the sight of her fear. 'None of these things were accidents. You can't have accidents, one after the other — happening just when anyone is there! When no one is out in the wing over our heads, nothing falls. When we are there, something happens. We come down here to look for Franz. We get in here, and without a second's pause, another fall blocks the door. Accident?' He laughed at her.

She stared, her eyes widening in horror.

'We should have seen somebody,' she whispered.

'We saw nobody. The ruins fell, the man was stolen, Franz has been taken, we are trapped — but nobody was there all the time. Nobody was seen, nobody made any marks, nobody made any sounds — '

'Franz heard them. I heard them,' she said, in a tiny voice.

'Did you?' he said, ironically. 'Then I'd say it was only because you were meant to hear, and be hooked like a stupid fish to go and have a look. Franz was hooked because you heard something you were meant to hear. When the corpse was stolen from the ruins, amidst all that muck, with beams balancing on dust, nothing moved, nothing fell over, nothing was heard, and no marks were left to show how they came, or where they went back.'

'You'll go mad if you think like that,' she said huskily.

'Perhaps that's what they mean,' he said. 'The madder we get the more we'll try and look for them, and the sooner we'll get trapped.'

'But they must be human!' she cried. 'They must be — '

'Why?' he demanded. 'Nothing they've done yet has been human. They've been unseen, unheard. They have not come near us. We can't touch them; they do not try to touch us. What's human about that?'

'What else can they be?'

He saw her shudder as she knelt there on the stone floor and she dropped her head as if ashamed of showing the weakness.

'There was a story once about this place being haunted,' he said, slowly.

'I know,' she said. 'But it was nonsense — village talk.'

'All right,' he said. 'So it was village talk, but it was useful for keeping nosey

203

parkers away all these years. It would be hellish funny if it turned out to be true.'

'It's nothing like that!' she said, suddenly angry. 'Franz said he was expecting them, but he was scared which side would get here first. I know that. Sometimes he used to tell me little things — not much — but enough to guess what he meant.'

'But suppose his friends were smugglers, whatever kind doesn't matter — what would the rivals be?'

She shook her head vigorously.

'Why should they hide and play a ghost game if they are so formidable that Franz was frightened of them *physically*?'

'He did not tell me!' She almost screamed the words out to stop him talking any more. 'It is no use trying to guess. Suppose we could look through the door and see what they are — what could we do?'

He signed to her to stop, then listened intently at the door. There was a movement outside, it was slight, could have been a piece of wreckage slithering in the dust, or a bird —

But suddenly he remembered that the birds had gone. It had not seemed important, but when they had come towards the house there had been birds everywhere, birds who seemed to have known that no one was there to disturb them. Then one or two had flown away, and after he and Kate had come out of the house again, there had been none at all. Their songs were far off in the trees, as if they had fled from the house, some instinct driving them away . . .

'Is there someone there?' she whispered, getting quickly to her feet.

Silence followed the slithering sound. He shrugged and turned to her.

'Could have been,' he said. 'I don't know.' He watched her quizzically. 'Are you fond of birds?'

'Birds?' She shook her head bewildered. 'Why?'

'They all went while we were up there,' he said.

She started and her eyes grew wider.

'They did that before,' she said.

'When the wing blew up?'

She nodded, too astonished to speak. 'How do you know that?'

'I'm guessing something now,' he said. 'When did they go? When did you notice they went?'

'It was late afternoon. I was in my room, and it seemed very quiet all of a sudden, and I saw some birds flying away, coming out of the eaves here. When they started to go, it was noisy, then it went quiet again. They all went.'

'They've all gone again now,' he said. 'Do you know why? Because the gas is coming again. The gas that blew up the wing.'

'What gas? How can — '

'Marsh gas. Fire damp. Methane,' he said. 'You get it in coal mines. Maybe there's a seam under here somewhere, and it's got a way up. My guess is it's being forced up by water down under us somewhere.'

'Will it — poison?'

'I don't know much about it,' Allison said. 'It kills birds. Canaries used to be used to test for it in mines.'

'It's coming up in here?'

'I don't know.'

She stared at him. He turned and began to go round the walls again, searching the cracks he found. He pointed to one near the ceiling.

'The light's coming in,' he said, turning back to her. 'I think — ' As he stepped to rejoin her his feet felt rocky on the floor, as if the flag moved on a pivot. He bent down, peering at the cracks which had held it secure at one time.

'Is it a trapdoor?' she said quickly.

'No. It's just been made loose by the building falling,' he said, straightening.

'We want a light — '

'No lights!' he said sharply. 'If there's any gas about here we needn't worry about finding an exit. We'll be blown through it.'

'Can you tell it's here?'

'No, but the birds went, and only a gas could have wrecked the wing like that. I'm guessing because I don't know, but it's worth being careful. The birds have gone.'

'They might have gone because — ' She stopped a moment. 'Because of what's out there! Animals know better than we do about unnatural things.'

'I know what you're thinking,' he said, searching the floor for a piece of iron he had seen earlier. 'But ghosts don't lift men and slam doors, nor start rocky buildings falling. Except — ' he added, remembering with a shock, ' — Poltergeists.'

He bent under the still and picked up the iron. It was a still spanner, heavy and crooked with slots at each end.

'Might make a hole,' he said, going back to the crack. 'Once you've got a hole you've got something you can make bigger.'

He put one end of the spanner in the crack near the ceiling and began to lever. Plaster dust and chips of bricks spurted out.

'This is going to take time,' he said gruffly. 'Keep an ear on the door.'

She went, but there was no sound beyond the door, and in the cellar there was only the scrunching noise of the spanner in the gap and the patter of pieces falling to the flags.

'This floor's rocky,' Allison said, pausing to wipe grit from his sweaty face. He bent and looked again. 'A light would be useful. Pity.'

He felt round the edges of the flag, then knelt down and tried to see details in the gloom.

'Suppose it's earth underneath?' she said.

For answer he put a knee on a corner of the stone and rocked it a fraction of an inch up and down.

'It sounds hollow,' he said. 'There could be a space under it. It's worth trying — if we can find a bit to lever it up by.

He tried the spanner in several places, but failed to get it in the crack. Angry at failure he stood up and trod heavily on the flag again. There was no doubt from the sound there was space underneath it. It was probably lack of support which had loosened the stone.

'The big cellar,' she said, coming up to him. 'It was deeper than this. It could be that underneath. This had only a few steps down. The other had a lot, and there was a kind of deep part in it which went under, like a fireplace. It could be that.'

'If it is then we'd be getting out of one trap into a bigger one,' he said.

'Remember, I heard something down there,' she said, in a very low voice. 'So there must be a way in or out of it still.'

He grinned.

'You've forgotten the poltergeists,' he said.

'It's worth trying,' she said.

'The light's coming from the crack up there,' he said, and went back to it. 'Better to chase the light than a knock from under.' He began to pull and scrunch at it again.

Slowly the crack widened, and the colour of the light became more distinct.

'Hell!' he said, almost choking.

'What is it?'

'It's the underneath of the cooker up there. This isn't light — it's fire!' He turned to her, face streaming with wet.

'Paper — rags — anything! Quick!' He tore off the remains of his tattered shirt, bundled it and stuffed it into the crack. As he did it, the bricks crumbled to one side, and his shirt went helplessly through to the firebars of the cooker. He drew it back again, coughing with the dust. 'Damn thing's white hot. If there's any gas building up here — '

She ran to him with armfuls of paper, straw wine cases. He looked at it, then ran his fingers through his hair.

'That's no good!' he gasped. 'I didn't realise it was so close — so white hot. Look! Look up there!'

She dropped the stuff and wiped her palms on the thighs of her trousers. She looked at him, her eyes glinting with the reflection of the glowing bars above.

'It's that stone, or it's nothing at all,' she said, huskily, and dropped to her knees and began digging at the dirt in the cracks with her fingers.

He went and smashed the side of a wooden crate with the spanner, getting a sliver from it three inches wide. He went back to the stone, put the wood to the crack and then began to drive it down with the heavy spanner.

She sat still, watching him, then looking past his sweating face to the glow of the fire in the crack.

'How does this gas come?' she said.

'It's heavy. It builds up from below.'

'Can you smell it?'

'I don't know.'

'There is a smell — oh, a sweet, horrible smell,' she said slowly.

He stopped working and sniffed.

'It's the barrel,' he said. 'It's never been cleaned out. It goes — '

He began to drive the wood deeper, then stopped knocking to try and use it as a lever, to force the crack wide enough to get the big spanner in.

'You don't believe that,' she said, and looked up at the glow of the fire.

The wood snapped in half, sheered to the level of the paving.

'If you could smell it, why would anybody take a canary to find it?' he said, angrily.

He went back to the crate and smashed more wood off it. He returned to the stone and drove another piece into the crack, gradually easing it wider. His breath rasped in his throat. She jumped to her feet, her hand to her neck.

'There's something here,' she said. 'I can feel it.'

'Soon the fire's going to feel it,' he said, desperately, and hammered another wedge into the crack. 'Wait! This is enough. Push the rest of that crate over.'

He got the crooked end of the spanner in the crack and tried to get a purchase on the stone with it. It would not grip. He tried to force the stone farther over still, using the spanner with all his strength. His breath was becoming painful, and sweat was blinding his eyes. She pushed the crate close to his side.

'It's coming!' he rasped suddenly. 'It's coming up. Better hold your breath as much as you can!'

Slowly the stone came up like an alligator's jaws, and when it was wide enough, he pushed part of the broken crate under it to hold it, and tossed the spanner with a clang to the floor. He straightened, gripped the edge of the stone with both hands and began to heave. She joined him on the other side, and slowly they pulled it up until it fell back with a crash against the wall. The hole where the fire showed grew larger with a sudden livid lightning crack in the shattered wall.

He looked at it an instant, then peered down. Dimly he could see a pile of crates and boxes directly below, as Kate had said, this must be the main cellar.

'Don't breathe more than you can help,' he gasped and grabbed her shoulder and pushed her down towards the hole.

She scrambled down and dropped in amongst the boxes. He followed. There was no longer any doubt the gas was there; it made itself felt in heavy breathing, in pain of the chest, in dizziness and uncertainty of their steps.

He pushed her ahead.

'This is the cellar,' she panted.

'Don't talk,' he said close to her ear.

He kept his hand on her arm as he drew her to the far side of the cellar away from the wine vault, tripping and stumbling on the boxes and old forgotten tools. The dim scene in the reflected fireglow had the background of nightmare. He felt the grip of something trying to steal his senses away, and keep him there, motionless until the fire became brilliant in one last, searing flash.

But he had been there before. Once more in the fleeting moments of mental drifting away from physical pain he saw the small boy, creeping in alarm and excitement in the old cellar.

There was a door in the corner. A tunnel beyond it. He had never dared go down it.

He crossed the dark place and fumbled for it in the blackness. She let herself be dragged along, rolling and bumping against him. She fell against the wall when he stopped to feel for the latch.

He found it and shoved it up, then broke his nails trying to grab hold to pull the rusted door open. He managed it, and turned. She had slid down, and was sitting against the wall like a beggar, head lolling. He bent, got her wrists and dragged her along the dirty floor in through the opening, bruising himself against the door and the sides of the tunnel, trying not to breathe and near bursting with pain for the need of breath. He got her clear of the door. From the tunnel he could just see the silhouette of the doorway from the glow of the distant fire.

The tunnel might have been fairly clear of gas, for the door had been shut tight. He reached forward, gripped the cross beams of it with his fingers and began to haul it, groaning, shut upon them.

There was no sound at first, just a brilliant, searing flash, a burst of Hell blazing in the narrowing gap of the closing door. The pressure of it slammed the door and threw him back along the tunnel. He crashed against a wall then fell to his knees. Then the world shook, and the roar of explosion came like the sheet-tin crash of thunder directly overhead.

He crouched there, stunned by noise and blinded by the light, all his other senses suspended in pain and shock. As his hearing returned he could hear rumbling and crashing, like thunder running away down the sky. It grew fainter and the trembling of the ground grew less, and finally there was silence, and he heard her gasping.

'I — can't breathe!' she whispered.

He crawled forward, feeling with his hand to where she lay in the pitch darkness. He felt her shoulder, put his hand round until he could lift her into a sitting position.

'Maybe the oxygen burnt up,' he said, but his voice had no real sound. 'Back end of a vacuum.'

He felt a strange relief that the explosion had come and gone. All they had to do was wait till the air came back, and they could gasp it in. He crouched there, holding her against him tightly.

He felt his brain melting again, drifting, and he held her more tightly still in the silent darkness. It was in the middle of what was nearly trance that he found himself gasping in great breaths; his body had found air before his senses.

An excitement surged up in him, and suddenly he realised her arms were round him, clutching him in desperation.

'It's come back!' he said, his voice hurting in his throat. 'It's come back!'

7

Darkness was absolute. There was no sound now but a faint drip of water, like an irregular ticking of a clock.

He stood up and felt his way along the wall. After a minute of doubt and indecision, he felt the back beams of the door.

'It's here,' he said, feeling for the latch.

'Is it a cupboard?' she said. 'I never saw it before.'

He pulled the latch down and pushed. Nothing happened. He put his shoulder to it. The rough wood burnt his bare skin, and the door stayed firm.

'Blocked,' he said, turning. 'Here. Where are you?'

He reached out into the darkness like a blind man, and suddenly touched her face. She reached up and caught his wrist.

'I won't let go,' she said.

He felt her shiver.

'What's the matter?' he said.

'If this is a cupboard — ' she whispered.

'We'll find out,' he said.

She held his wrist beside her. He felt his way along the wall with his right hand. They went forward, pace after pace, and with each one, their breathing became freer, their tenseness less.

'It goes on — somewhere,' he said.

'What is it, then?'

'It could be an old bolt hole, I suppose. But not for the present house — or what's left of it now.'

Pace by pace, and still his fingers, touching just ahead, found no blocking wall. He went on talking, like whistling in the dark.

'The house was built about 1790, I guess, but there was probably one here before. A long time ago. A bolt hole would be often a part of an old house, and used during the civil wars and religious festivals of intolerance. In fact, they were often necessary . . . '

'Where would it go, then?'

'If it is a bolt hole it would come up somewhere clear of the house. The wall feels like brick.'

'The air smells fresh,' she said.

'And it came in quickly after the burn up,' he said. 'So there must be an opening somewhere.'

On and on, bumping against each other and wiping the rough walls with their arms, and still no light no break in the absolute blackness.

'Stop,' she said. 'I'm tired. I could fall down.'

They stopped and she let go his wrist. They stayed in silence for what seemed a long time, and then he began to laugh softly.

'Why are you laughing?' she said.

'I was going to say, 'Look at me',' he said. 'But just think of me. Stripped, filthy, beaten, burnt, lost in a place that could be the seam of some long forgotten mine; back in a house that used to be a dream, fighting for a princess that's come true, but hardly as I thought it would. Yesterday, I never thought of that. Yesterday I was strict and smart and busy and respected, bowler hat and Bentley, offices on the pavement — Now that's all gone as if *that* — not this — is the dream. I can feel this is real because it hurts. The other was a fear, fear of not being respected, fear of being found out, fear of people pointing, fear of not having money . . . '

'You're not a coward,' she said.

'I stood and watched him hit you,' he said. 'I was frightened of being hurt any more. I haven't changed.' He reached out and touched her. 'Let's get on.'

They began the slow, stumbling walk again, saying nothing for a long while.

'Suppose it is — part of a mine?' she said. 'We might not get out of it. The air might be coming down a shaft somewhere.'

'What's the good of guessing?' he snapped angrily. 'There's no other way. We've got to get on!'

The way seemed endless. Often they stopped in the darkness to listen, but there was only the faint drip of water, echoing in the tunnel.

'That dripping doesn't seem to be

getting much farther away,' she said, and he felt her muscles tense.

'It might be echo,' he said. 'A tunnel's like a speaking tube.'

But she could detect uncertainty in his voice.

'Stop. Stop again,' she said, desperately. 'I can't go on like this, just going — nowhere, hearing that drip — I — '

He stopped and she stumbled against him, clutching him hard against her.

'I'm scared,' she whispered. 'I'm dead scared. I've had enough.'

He put his arms round her and they stayed hugging together like frightened animals in the impenetrable darkness.

'Am I a princess?' she whispered urgently. 'Am I? Am I?'

'Yes, yes. I told you.'

She began to cry very quietly, and clung to him desperately. He remembered her, bold and unafraid when he had first seen her on the rock. But as the fire in him rose, so did jealousy and he saw Franz again, sullenly scowling in the darkness.

'You hurt me!' she said suddenly. It was like a little cry.

He let her go suddenly, pushed her away from him and got her wrist.

'Come on,' he said roughly. 'We've got to get on.'

She pulled him back.

'No,' she said, desperately. 'No!'

'We've got to get on,' he said again.

'I can't,' she whispered. 'My foot. I can't.'

'For goodness sake!' he snarled. 'What's the matter? Your foot?'

'It hurts too much,' she said.

He bent right down felt her foot and the ankle. He could feel a swelling around the joint.

'I think it was when we fell in through the door,' she said. 'I don't know. I was nearly out.'

She leant against the invisible wall.

'You go on,' she said. 'Perhaps, when you find the way, you can come back.'

He crouched there in the darkness.

'If I don't find a way, I'd sooner be with you,' he said, standing again. 'Better do it like the firemen.' He bent. 'Get over my shoulder.'

While she did it, he kept his right hand

on the opposite wall so as not to lose his sense of direction.

'You can't go far like this,' she said.

He straightened, staggering slightly, and began to go on slowly.

'If only we had light,' he gasped. 'Just a glim.'

'It's no good,' she said. 'Let me down.'

'I'm not going to lose you,' he said, his voice grating.

They went on through the slow dripping silence.

'Let me down,' she said again. 'I could walk a bit.'

He let her down against the wall and stood, his chest heaving with long, slow breaths.

'Lean on me then,' he panted. 'Take the weight off it.'

They went on again, hobbling blindly through the dark until she stopped again from pain.

'The water dripping,' she said. 'It's louder.'

'We haven't doubled back anywhere,' he said, and leaned back against the wall. He pawed sweat from his face. 'It must be part of the mine. A tunnel wouldn't be this long.'

She let her back slide down the wall until she was squatting on the ground. He dropped on to his heels, resting his hands on the floor and breathing deeply.

'Go on alone,' she said softly. 'We can't go any further like this.'

'If it's a mine,' he said, ignoring her, 'there might be other galleries, but there haven't been any opening on the right.'

'Have we been going down?'

'We could have been going any way,' he said. 'Upside down, sideways — wouldn't make any difference in this blackout.'

He turned and sat beside her against the wall. He felt for her hand and found it.

'I don't think I can go on much longer,' he said, and squeezed her hand.

'We'll go on — soon,' she said.

They sat in the total darkness listening to the steady drip of the water. The feeling that this was the end of it, that they would never get out of this place again seized him in a terrible grip.

She turned and put her shoulder against his chest. He put his arms round her and hugged her against him, desperately. They sat for a long time, as if he used the last flow of his strength in holding her to him.

Sleep came for a while, the dreamless dark of exhaustion. When he awoke there was only sensation of her body against him, for he could see nothing and for a moment pain was numbed and the dripping of the water had become a pattern in his brain, no longer noticed until he searched for it.

Then he heard her whisper, and he realised that it was a whisper that had penetrated sleep and brought him to his senses.

'There is something moving,' she breathed. 'Can you hear?'

He listened. The water drip pattern came to the fore, trying to kill his hearing for anything else, but gradually he heard a series of soft, rhythmic groaning sounds. They seemed far distant.

She moved away from him and he sat up rigidly, listening.

227

'What is it?' she said.

'Can't make out,' he said.

They listened. The soft groaning sound was repeated five or six times, then stopped.

'Footsteps?' she said.

He felt her shiver.

'No,' he said. 'No, it couldn't be that. Listen. There it is again.'

They listened to the soft groaning. It seemed to be coming from all directions at once as the tunnel mixed and confused the echoes.

'Could it be any more of these — things?' she whispered.

'I don't know about things. It sounds quite definite. Something solid . . . What was the sound you heard in the hall before Franz went?'

'Like that,' she said. 'But not so plain. I didn't recognise it at first. I do now.'

'Then it must be coming from back towards the house,' he said. 'But the end's blocked, and we passed no opening.'

'There wasn't any on my side. I was propping myself against the wall most of the way. I would have known if the wall stopped anywhere.'

'Perhaps there was a hole in the roof,' he said.

There was silence for a time, then the groaning began again.

He got up. She put a hand round his ankle and held it in case she should lose him in the dark. But he stood straight and put his hand above his head.

'The roof's only a foot up,' he said. 'We ought to go back. Where the sound is, there's a hole, and a hole is what we need now. We can't go on and on. We might be going round in circles in some mine gallery.'

She hauled herself up by his leg, and he put his arm round her for support when she straightened.

'It isn't so bad,' she said. 'I could try for a way.'

They started back, slowly, lamely, and as they went each felt a greater physical strain than they had known before. She stopped and leaned against the wall, gasping.

'Sorry, it seems to be — worse

229

somehow,' she said.

'Know why?' he said. 'We're going uphill. That's why it was easy coming down.'

He was glad to stop and let his arm fall. It was numbed with dragging along the room over his head. They stayed a minute, listening.

'It's louder,' he said.

As soon as he spoke, it stopped again.

'I'll carry you again,' he said, after a while. 'You keep your hand on the ceiling if you can.'

'All right.'

The quickness of her agreement made him realise that the sound had brought hope into the pit.

He lifted her again and stood straight.

'Can you touch it?'

'Yes.'

They went slowly along through the darkness and the increasing pressure on his lungs told him how steep the climb really was. The sound ceased altogether. There was only his heavy breathing, the shuffling footfalls, the faint dragging of her fingers on the roof, and in the distance the insane beat of the dripping water.

'Wait!' Her voice was like a little gasp.

He staggered to a halt.

'Something there?' he panted.

'Yes.' He let her down and reached up. His hand met no roof. He felt round and made out the rounded edge of an opening there, and then gave a shout. 'Rungs!' he cried. 'Iron rungs. I can feel one, two — They go up!'

'The noise — ?' she said.

They stood listening, but the groaning had ceased.

'It's like something moving now and again,' she said. 'Like when the wind blows.'

Suddenly the sound came, more clearly now, so that they could hear a thin squeak with the groaning.

'That's it, then,' he said, wiping his face with his hand. 'We go up.'

He lifted her and held her while she fumbled to find the rungs in the shaft above. At last she began to lift up out of his grip.

'Okay,' she said. Her voice echoed in the shaft.

'Keep on going up,' he said. 'I'm coming close behind.'

They climbed for a minute or more, going very slowly, fumbling for the next hold, and then suddenly she let out a little cry.

'Light!' she said. 'I can see light!'

'Are you at the top?'

She did not answer for a moment. He heard her gasping and then a scrabbling sound.

'Yes,' she called back.

He clambered up the last rungs and hauled himself over the brick edge of the shaft. There was a pin-point of light that might have been a little hole nearby, or a tunnel mouth a mile away. His sight could not adjust itself. He rolled over and lay on his back on the damp brick, hands on his stomach, getting breath. She knelt beside him, staring at the pinpoint.

'Light,' she breathed. 'I was beginning to think I was blind.'

'You'll see in a minute,' he said, and got up.

Slowly they began to see faint objects in the pin of light. The groaning started again, close by.

'Water,' he said. 'A boat!'

Faintly they could see what looked like the end of an underground backwater, with an old boat, rotted and half full of water, grunting disconsolately against the timber of the stage when faint, occasional surges disturbed the surface.

Overhead a brick tunnel arched, and there were items of old wood and iron equipment lying about the landing stage, rotting. Abandoned long ago, perhaps only disturbed by adventurous children in later years. The boat was still, then a faint wave came towards the stage, rolling in the pin-point of light and the wood groaned once more.

'There's certainly a way out of here,' he said. 'This must be a backwater from the lake. Once there was a canal out of it, on the pine forest side. It all dried up and overgrew long before I came here as a boy. They got the coal away by water, a hundred years ago. Can you walk?'

He helped her up.

'It's not so bad now I can see,' she said, leaning on him, and smiled. 'I thought we were lost, down there.'

They began to walk slowly along the stage beside the water and the grey light ahead grew stronger, but the tunnel curved and they could not see the end of it. Once or twice there were soft splashes where rats slipped into the canal and little, oily waves rolled by on the top of the water. The light began to get a greenish colour, and they came round the gradual bend in the tunnel and saw the source of it.

The end of the tunnel showed light filtered by dense overgrown bushes and trees. And standing against the green mass was the grill of iron bars closing the tunnel mouth.

'Wait here,' he said, staring at it. 'I'll go and look.'

She leant against the curving tunnel wall and he went ahead to where the bars ended the stage like a portcullis, and further over he could see their teeth going down into the water, shimmering in deep green. Old chains and massive padlocks held it fast. When the mine had been finally abandoned, perhaps someone had meant to come back.

He went to her.

'It's locked up there, but there's a gallery off to the left here — ' he pointed, ' — we'll have to try it.'

She nodded, leaned against him again and they went towards the grille as far as a gallery opening on the left. The ground under their feet was hard with dried mud and dust and uneven, rusty rails of a truck railway curved out of the opening and ran along the edge of the stage.

They turned into the gallery. Some light was coming into it from an opening some way down it. They could see the crooked lines of the railway running along to where a little train of old trucks stood waiting for miners who would not come any more. They stood where the tunnel bent round, about fifty yards away.

'Let me rest a minute,' she said, breathlessly, and winced. 'It's every now and again it gets bad — '

She sat down against the wall and

began to massage her swollen ankle. He leaned against the tunnel side.

'The man who came,' he said. 'The dead man. Was he the only one who came there?'

'While I was there.' She nodded.

'Why did he come?'

'He had business with Franz.' She went on rubbing the ankle. 'I don't know what it was.'

'What sort of a man was he?'

'Nice,' she said, looking up.

In the gloom he started to laugh.

'Your face,' he said. 'It's black as a sweep's.'

She laughed. 'So is yours. But we shall be out soon.'

He squatted on his heels and put out a hand to her ankle.

'Let me feel,' he said. 'I remember a bit about it.' He touched it gently, looking for a breakage, then shook his head. 'It's still solid. Nothing broken.'

He squatted there, looking at her.

'You're the most beautiful black-faced girl I ever saw,' he said. 'Did the man think so, too?'

'I hadn't a black face,' she said, and stared curiously. 'Why do you say that?'

'You said he was nice, so I think he paid you some attention,' he said.

Far away in the tunnel the old boat groaned a few more times.

'He looked as if he would.' she said. 'He tried very hard to — catch my eye.'

'You didn't let him?'

'I did,' she said, cocking her head. 'I like to flirt, and it was lonely, waiting there.'

'Do you know where he came from?'

She shook her head. For a moment she looked up towards the train of trucks, then back to him.

'I don't like this place. It frightens me.'

'We'll find a way out soon,' he said, but made no move to get up. His eyes narrowed. 'You're thinking of Franz again.'

Her eyes started wide.

'Yes,' she said. 'I can't help it.' She reached out and gripped his arm. 'We've got to try and find him!'

Her voice echoed queerly in the tunnel,

and both realised that they had been talking in whispers almost, as if the unseen might hear them. Allison looked swiftly towards the water, as if someone there might be watching.

'I'm getting the creeps again,' he said. 'Sometimes I think light's worse than dark. Perhaps because you can see what isn't there.'

He wiped his face with his hands, and the black streaked with the sweat breaking out again.

'Why do you still think Franz is alive?' he said, meaning to hurt. 'We've been lucky. They tried to tip the ruins on us, and they tried to blow us up in the wine cellar. We've got away twice. Do you think he could be as lucky as that?'

She stared through him, her eyes hurt.

'He mustn't be dead,' she whispered.

He bent close to her, watching her savagely.

'You love me,' he said tensely. 'You know that now. I know it.'

She looked at him steadily, her grey-green eyes like diamonds in the greenish light.

'Yes,' she said.

'And I love you,' he said, taking her shoulder and gripping till it hurt. 'That's all that matters. Franz doesn't matter. If he's dead or if he's alive, it doesn't matter. Forget him!'

She dropped her head.

'I can't,' she said. 'You don't understand — '

'Why don't I?' he cried. 'How can he matter? He's over — he's past! Forget him!'

She shivered suddenly and covered her face with her hands. He squatted there, eyes alight with fury, as if he wanted to hit her. He controlled himself, and fist clenched he stood up and walked to the water tunnel. He stood there, his back to her, eyes closed, trying to reason what kind of madness made her like this.

How could she love one and want the other?

Deliberately he tried to think the worst of her; the way she had tried to bait him, the way she had challenged him with her sex; the strange contempt of those early moments, and the ready admission of the

239

sexual attraction between them. But that hardness was only like an added allure to the girl he knew now, as if she were more than one, had faces that could change as she wanted. But he knew the one that was real; the one that showed what he wanted to know.

Again he wiped his face, then turned back. She was sitting there against the wall, just staring at nothing. Compassion as well as love made him falter in his anger.

He squatted down again.

'You've been through it,' he said.

She looked round at him.

'We,' she said.

He wanted to touch her, feel her body against his again, drive Franz out of her mind.

'I'm better now,' she said. 'Help me up.'

He did so, and saw her wince as she put weight on the swollen ankle.

'I'll carry you,' he said.

He lifted her across his chest.

'Isn't the fireman easier?' she said, putting her arm round his neck.

'I want to hold you,' he said, and crushed her against him as he began to walk slowly along the uneven floor between the old rails.

The light seemed to get worse. Fear walked behind him again. He stopped and looked back towards the water.

'One of those rats, perhaps,' he said.

'It sounded bigger,' she said in a whisper.

Once again the feeling that they were being watched and shadowed became too strong to be ignored. He let her down suddenly and she stood against the wall, her aching foot lifted clear of the floor. In that instant he knew that she would not walk any more until the pain had gone.

'Wait here,' he said quietly. 'I'll make sure.'

He went quickly down the tunnel between the rails, and as he did he heard a chunking sound. He stopped, unable to tell whether it came from in front or behind him. The strange echoes in the tunnels destroyed the sense of direction.

He looked back, saw her leaning against

241

the wall, and his eyes travelled to the little train curving round out of sight beyond her. Instinctively he felt something was wrong; something had changed in the scene, but he could not tell what it was.

Again there was a chunking sound, but this time it came from the ground on which he stood. He stared down incredulously. There was no opening, just the dirt and the old rails. He scraped dirt aside with his foot in case there was a trapdoor behind it, but there was only stone.

Once more the sound came, and suddenly he knew.

It was travelling along the rails. He looked quickly to the truck train on the bend. The chunk came again and then a deep rumble that trembled the rails so that dirt between them began to shift.

'The train — '

She gave a little scream, turned to run towards him, but the ankle gave at the first step and she went down between the rails. He ran back towards her, seeing the train gathering speed, filling the tunnel with a rumble of fearful thunder, growing to a deafening pitch as it ran down towards Kate.

She struggled to get up and got to her knees when he reached her. She put her arms out to him as he bent, grabbed her and swung her up into his arms. Only a few yards away the train rocked and thundered down towards them, the ground beneath his feet beating to the clack rhythm of the wheels on the crooked lines.

He turned and began to run, slowly, heavily, deafened by the thunder of the train bearing down on him, the groaning roar and rattle of chains.

He ran, praying that he would not trip on an uncovered tie between the rails. His steps were slow, with tiredness and the double weight he had the growing feeling that soon his legs must give way altogether, and they would go down and be smashed and ripped to pieces by the iron train.

It roared behind him like the screaming of animals in wild pursuit. The deafening row was coming from behind and all around him, like a solid attack, trying to make him let go and fall before it. Breath came no more, but stopped in his throat.

He heard her give a little scream, hardly audible in the unholy din and hugged her desperately against him as if she might help his dragging weakening steps.

The end of the tunnel came, and as he staggered to one side his foot caught in the curving rail and he reeled in an effort not to fall backwards. The edge of a truck, swinging round the curve, hit him glancingly and sent him tottering clear of the train. He fell against the wall, holding her to him, panting as if his lungs would burst, trying to think what was happening while the devils of noise dinned in his ears like a physical pain.

The trucks rumbled round alongside the water, rocking and heeling with their speed, and then went groaning and rattling, slower and slower, up the slight braking incline where once they had stood to tip into the waiting barges.

The train halted with a rattle and

clank of chains, but the echoes of its career seemed still to beat in his ears. He just stood against the wall, holding her to him as desperately as she clung round his neck.

'I'll kill them,' he gasped. 'I'll kill them!'

Disturbed by the earthquake of the train, the derelict boat began to rub and grunt like an old man laughing. He set her down against the wall and went back to the tunnel mouth.

'Don't go!' she whispered, her voice dried up with horror. 'They'll kill you! Don't go!'

He turned to her and brought the little pistol from his pocket. He bent and put it into her hand.

'This'll keep you company,' he said.

'Don't go!' she whispered.

'It's no good waiting and let them have another shot,' he said. 'I've got to find them now.'

He went into the rail tunnel and began to move swiftly along it. The light grew dim. The only movement was the faint glowing from the uneasy water behind him, reflecting on the rounded brick roof. He came to the turn in the tunnel where the trucks had stood. It was sharper than he thought, and darkness increased beyond it. He saw the crooked rails fading into the blackness ahead of him. Nothing moved.

He knew that someone was there in the darkness; someone who was hiding from him. He ran forward suddenly, making little sound on the thick coaldust between the rails. The darkness increased, but he could see the shadows of props and strutting for the roof beams. Brickwork had ended. He was entering the gallery leading to the main shaft.

The props stood like a little forest in the gloom. He stopped and searched the darkness carefully, then looked back. There was only a faint glow from the bend in the tunnel; not enough to show him up to anyone deeper in the tunnel.

He went forward again, listening. Far off he heard the boat grunt. His slow-moving foot kicked something that dragged in the dust. He bent and picked it up. It was a piece of wood, heavy and about two feet long. He gripped it hard, like a club, and the feel of being armed made him more angry, more determined. He went on through the gloom. The tunnel broadened and he saw old winding wheels and gears.

The shaft was somewhere just ahead of him. In a line to his left another small train of trucks stood. He stole into the gloom, and amongst the props he saw other openings, probably loading bays for the trucks near the central shaft into which chains hung down and disappeared.

There were a hundred places for men to hide. The place was a labyrinth.

He stopped again, listening, but there was little noise. Somewhere water dripped, but there was no sound of man.

Somewhere in the darkness there was a way out of this place; but hidden there were perhaps a dozen other ways that would lead only into greater darkness and to despair and death.

As he stood in the silence, an idea came to him; an idea that changed the whole mystery of this place round.

As if he had watched the face of a clock, wondering why the hands moved, then suddenly saw through to the gears inside it.

He wiped his face with his hand, gripped the wood stave more tightly and stood a moment more, listening. Then he turned and went silently back along the tunnel, treading the thick dust between the tracks.

As he went back into the place of the water he saw her leaning against the wall, standing now, the gun pointing directly at him.

She stopped and let the gun-hand fall to her side, then drew a gasping breath.

'You,' she said. 'Thank heaven. What did you find?'

'Nothing,' he said. 'There is a way out through there, but it's one of a dozen ways in. We can't risk it. We'd starve in there.'

'But there's no way back!' she said.

'There may be a way out,' he said.

He looked towards the green-lit grille of iron bars and the crooked iron tracks leading up to it. He turned his back to her and looked at the switch points, where the curve from the shaft tunnel joined the loading track.

He left her and went back to where the trucks stood on the level above the incline which had stopped them. He looked around amongst the rotting, rusty equipment that was piled about anyhow.

He got a pick, tested the head on the haft, then came back to the points. It took five minutes to shift the once moving part of the iron across so that the track led straight along the waterside. He went back to the truck train, put his shoulder to the end truck and pushed it towards the decline.

The train grunted, but did not move more than an inch before it stopped again. He stood back, breathing hard, and then fetched an iron crowbar from the old forgotten tool heap. He got it between the truck wheel and the track and put his weight on the end.

The train grunted, rattled with chains, and went forward three inches. He repeated the operation and gained six inches. Each time he did it, the weight needed was less. The leading truck had gone over on to the decline, then the follower. When the two were on the down grade the two still level, he threw down the crowbar and put his shoulder to the end truck.

The train grunted, shifted, and then began the low rumble which had sounded like the thunder of death in the tunnel.

He stood back, panting, and watched the heavy old iron train gather speed down the gentle slope. The trucks began to rock on the uneven track, and the tunnel filled with the rattle and roar of its going. He saw Kate put her hands to her ears as the train rumbled past her and headed on towards the iron bars at the tunnel mouth.

The train struck with a crash that shook the very floor. Bricks started cracks in the roof and began to fall. The mirror surface of the water suddenly shifted and stirred into a frenzied agitation then burst into foam as one truck toppled and dropped into the water, trying to drag the others with it.

The sounds died slowly, echoes seemed

to last for minutes after, and he ran through the thunderous noise as the wrecked train settled, the leading part halfway through the smashed bars of the gate, the rest hanging into the water.

He swung her up in his arms and carried her to the broken gateway. He ducked and sawed his way between the reaching branches of little trees beside the canal.When they had got a little way along, he set her down. The sun was hot, making the young leaves brilliant green. Birds sang shrilly above them. The canal, reflecting green and black streaks of branches, vanished beyond an overhanging mass of willow. On the left of the canal path a bank, thick with small trees and bushes led up towards the line of blue sky.

'Never thought I'd see that again,' he said.

She leant her back against a twisted little tree trunk, and caught his arm in a sudden fearful grip.

'What are you going to do?' she said, watching him in slow horrified understanding.

'Going back to the house — what's left of it,' he said.

'No. We've got away so far. Let's get right away now! There's no sense in going back!'

'Look, if we run,' he said slowly, 'we leave a pack of hounds behind us. That's not for me any more. They've been following, watching, and they'll go on doing it, if we don't find out who they are. We can't go on hour after hour, knowing that someone it waiting right behind us — '

'No!' she said, shaking her head wildly. 'You don't understand what you're doing. You don't understand them. Let's get out of here now. Right away. Now!'

He looked at her steadily.

'To where?' he said ironically. 'You're wanted for a murder, didn't you say? And where I come from, they'll be pleased to see me for one reason only . . . First, let's get further away from here.'

He carried her again until the bank sloped down and joined the path by the canal. Then he turned, seeing the gleam of the lake water ahead of him, until his back was towards the reflected gleams of the water on the arching leaves of the trees above.

'Don't go back!' she said, starting to struggle. 'Don't go back!'

Again he put her down, this time in the crutch of an old tree.

'You've got to go back,' he said. 'There's somebody calling for you soon.'

'I can't go back any more,' she said, her head falling into her hands. 'I can't go back!'

He leant against the tree, looking down at her.

'Do you know why I gave up looking in that mine shaft?' he said. 'Do you know why I came back to you?'

She shifted her face abruptly. It was black with coaldust and streaked with tears, yet nothing of this could cover the sudden alarm and tension in her expression.

'Why?' she whispered.

He leant closer.

'They've been aiming at you as well as me,' he said. 'Which means only one thing; you know something and they're afraid you've told me. That's why they'll follow and follow until — '

'If they're following, why don't you care any more?' she challenged.

'They always keep hidden. They always use dark places,' he said. 'There's a reason for that, the same reason that they won't show themselves in the broad day-light.'

He watched her, and went on:

'I don't believe the story you told, Kate. I don't believe you found Franz as a friend who would help you in your trouble. I believe that Franz was part of the plot. I think that somewhere you killed a man — maybe by accident — and that you had to run back here to hide with Franz until you could get away. I believe that you set out from here to start with.

'I believe that you came into this place the same way as you meant to leave it. I believe that your friends came for you last night, but because I was here, Franz had to warn them with the lamp on the lake, and that they went away again — '

'No!' It was a startled little gasp of horror.

'I'm sure of it,' he said. 'I'm sure that my guess was right that somewhere down in the old mine workings is a flooded way through from the lake to the open sea, and that's the way you came, and the way your friends have gone.'

Her hands pressed against her mouth. Her eyes were big, watching him as if he might be some executioner. Slowly she controlled her hysteria.

'Why did you come here?' she said.

'I told you. I came because it was a place of escape, not physically, but mentally.'

'There must have been another reason.'

He hesitated a long time.

'The man who died in the first explosion,' he said at last. 'I knew him. Many years ago. When I saw him lying there these few hours back, and knew him, I didn't feel a shock, or surprise. It was as if I knew it already. In fact, I did know it already.'

'How could you know? How?' Fear

and suspicion was growing bright in her eyes.

'He and I were little boys in the village here. We grew up to the age of twelve together. We were best friends. There was nobody else. It was always he and I. And there was a funny little thing that we got used to as time went on.

'If ever we wanted to meet, we didn't call for each other where we lived. We didn't have to. We just went to that rock overhanging the lake here, and in a little while, the other one would come.

'One day he didn't come. and I knew that he was hurt. I went to his cottage, and his mother told me he had been knocked down by a car. I seemed to know it already, for I could feel the pain in my leg, and he had broken his.

'I told my mother about it, one day, I suppose, it frightened me. She told me to get a book from the library called *The Corsican Brothers*. It was a story of two brothers who were such friends, that when one died, the other knew and came back to avenge him.

'When Jim got better, it became

256

our secret. I lent the book to him. Afterwards, the acuteness of each other's senses became quite strong.

'Then suddenly they moved away. When he was going, we solemnly swore we would know what happened to each other, that we would be forever like the Corsican Brothers.

'But he went, and we forgot each other. I heard of him only once since then, Kate. Only once.'

'When?' The word was sharp as a snake's hiss.

'It comes after,' he said. 'The night he died, I had a dream not about him, but about this place and the rock. I was in a state of mental turmoil, guilt and frustration. I could have dreamt anything that could have meant an escape back to the guiltless times of boyhood. When I woke, I knew I would have to come here. I thought it was just to escape, perhaps to fake a suicide in the bottomless lake — yes, that was in my mind, but I tried not to recognise it.

'Then, when I saw him, it hit me — not the shock of finding him dead — but the shock of knowing that he was dead. It could have been coincidence, Kate. Coincidence that I came here when he was dead, but I feel it wasn't. You see, I'd never seen him since the day we made the vow, over twenty years ago, that we would always know what happened to the other, and we would come to the other's rescue. That was the childish angle, Kate, but perhaps the boy in us never dies. Perhaps the imagination and the adventure and the pure affection for a friend can last even through the suffocation of a killing civilisation. I don't know. All I believe is that I did somehow know that Jim was dead that night, and it was that which brought me back here to find something. I thought it was boyhood and innocence I wanted to find. I think now that it was Jim calling me back. You see, Kate, such has been my life of push and fighting and senseless ambition, that I never made a friend after Jim went out of my life.'

'When — did you hear about him?' She whispered now, as if she knew the answer.

'Quite by accident once I heard that

he was in the Special Branch at Scotland Yard. I don't even know whether it was true or not. But, Kate, I believe that he followed you here. And I believe that's why Franz killed him.'

'He did not say he was from *them*,' she breathed.

'What did he say?'

'He said he came because it was a place he had known very long ago,' she said, eyes staring into the distance. 'He wanted to look round.'

'He went to the dining-room,' Allison went on for her. 'He went to see the picture that would identify Franz and give the clue to the way you and the other agents were getting in and out of the country.

'Franz had found the methane leak. While you flirted with Jim, Franz ducted it in to the old dining-room. Fairly easy to do that when he knew where the crack was the gas was coming out of. He closed the shutters of the room and fixed them so that they could not be opened from the inside. He cut the canvas from the frame in case his plan didn't quite go off.

'It was a hot day. Jim flirted with you in his shirt-sleeves, his jacket lying somewhere. Franz had only to see that he had no torch, in the jacket, only matches, then he came and found you.

'He acted the jealous lover and dragged you off, right away from the house.

'Jim was left where he wanted to be, and walked into the trap.'

She gave a violent shudder.

'He should not have been killed,' she moaned. 'Franz would not have done that. It was an accident. It must have been!'

'Franz must have guessed who he was, but the trap was like this. Jim, like I, knew where that picture had been. If he was not a detective, he wouldn't have gone in that dark room and struck a match to find the picture. Franz got his proof and his security in one shot.'

She looked at him pleading.

'I didn't know that,' she said. 'I swear I didn't know that. I thought it was an accident. The house was old and could have fallen. I didn't know about the gas.'

'I don't think Franz knew just what kind of a bang it was going to make,' Allison said.

'If Franz did it — he has paid for it!' she cried desperately. 'You know he must be dead. We should have found him. We should have heard him!'

'Perhaps they were luckier with him than they were with us,' he snapped. 'Maybe it's saved him trouble.'

Again jealousy rose and overshadowed his anger.

'He could have helped us!' she said, blazing suddenly. 'He knows the way to escape. He knows our friends. You don't. You can do nothing!'

'Oh yes, I can, Kate,' he said, and smiled slowly.

'What can you do, then?'

'I can go back to the house,' he said.

'No!'

'Yes,' he said. 'Better come with me, Kate. You might not be safe — alone!'

He went to take her up again, but she fought him off, breathless and determined.

'I'm not going back there!'

261

'I'm taking you back,' he said quietly. 'Remember you can't go anywhere else. You need a carrier.'

She smacked his face.

'Don't laugh at me!' she said, between her teeth.

'I can't help it,' he said. 'Your face is as black as a sweep's!'

Suddenly she put her hands to her face. In that moment he picked her up. She beat his shoulders with her fists, she recovered and stayed still in his arms as he began to walk.

'I don't want to go back,' she said. 'Please!'

'I've got to go back,' he answered. 'So you have, too.'

8

They stooped at a tumbling stream coming down fern-banked rocks, and washed and drank. When they had done, he picked her up again and went on towards the house. Her body was stiff and resisting for a moment, then she gave way.

They came to a break in the little trees and saw the house. One wing still remained, but the central part, where the kitchen had been, was badly damaged now, and rafters stuck up from the broken centre roof like the bones of a whale skeleton. The birds were back, as if nothing had happened.

He stopped by the open stable, watching the house. He felt her shiver slightly as he held her against him, then he turned and carried her in by the car. He set her down and opened the car door.

'Sit down and wait for me,' he said.

'What are you going to do?' she asked tensely.

'Look round,' he said, and glanced back at her. 'Still got that pistol?'

She nodded.

'Whatever happened to the keys?' he said suddenly. and nodded towards the dashboard.

He sounded almost casual, and she looked wary.

'I took them,' she said. Her eyes changed, the suspicion softened and the light in them became intense and pleading. 'Don't go in there,' she whispered urgently, catching his arm. 'Let's get away altogether. Let's get away!'

'They would follow,' he said. 'And how would we get by in a car like this, the girl with a dirty old remnant of a shirt and the man with no shirt at all. It's silly little things like that you have to remember. We'd have to get some clothes — borrow some — anything, but they're necessary.'

She kept holding his arm.

'There must be some in there,' he said.

She nodded abruptly.

'Yes. Remember my room? There is a

264

bag there, ready packed in the cupboard. Franz — ' Her voice stumbled on the name, 'had some in the next room. But don't — '

'We must have them,' he said quietly. 'We couldn't even go and buy any, in the state we're in.'

She pulled the little gun out of her pocket and put it in his hand.

'You have it,' she said. 'I'll wait here. I promise.'

He held the gun lightly, but remained looking down at her.

'You're very beautiful,' he said. 'You don't look like a murderess. You didn't deliberately kill anyone.'

'I did not mean to when I went, but I meant to when I was there,' she said, and frowned. 'It was a very simple matter. I went to see a man, and he started to blackmail me. He thought he would have his way. I lost my temper, got his gun and shot him.'

He watched her, knowing some great struggle with truth was surging inside her.

'I heard of no shootings lately,' he said curiously.

She drew a deep breath.

'It happened in an Embassy,' she said. 'Sacred ground, you know.'

As he watched her she looked away and he saw tears start in her eyes. He knew they were for Franz, and the flood of jealousy ripped through him. He pushed himself away from the car, his face suddenly taut and angry.

'Wait,' he said, and went out on to the cobbles.

He glanced back a moment. She sat there staring at him, eyes bright as diamonds with tears, both hands to her mouth to stop herself calling him back.

He went on towards the building. As he came near it he slowed. The centre part of the building had collapsed, and the kitchen was a mass of rafters and rubble.

He tried to remember his exploits of years ago, and recalled a stairway at the far end of the wing.

He turned to his left and went quickly and quietly along the grass, watching the blank windows of the house above him. He had the feeling that someone watched from behind that blankness but he could see nothing. The birds spun about in the air, swooping, then perching on the gutter, chirruping as if there was nothing to fear in that silent house.

He came to the end of the house where there had once been a window with a loose catch. As he tried it, he remembered the very first time, and the breathless adventure of finding the catch give way and knowing the whole house stood open to him.

The catch was stiff now, but gave in the same way. He pushed up the sash and climbed in at the window.

He stood a moment in the empty room of cobwebs and dust, listening. Somewhere water was hissing and bubbling, probably from a broken pipe.

He went out and looked along the corridor. It was dark now, where the end had collapsed, yet the floor above was still standing. He crossed it and went slowly up the narrow, servant's stairs, where the wood creaked and grunted under his weight.

At the top he turned and looked back

quickly, as if to surprise someone who might be behind him. He looked down empty stairs.

The feeling that there was something unnatural about this hideous pursuit came back in full force, and for a moment he was afraid again. The moment passed for he knew the force behind the collapse, behind moving Jim's body, behind letting the train of trucks go, was human. It could not have been anything else. Ghosts don't set broken walls rocking, nor unset the brakes on trucks.

He went quickly past the old unused rooms on the first floor. Their doors were still open, their curtains of webs still unbroken by any human passage through them.

He went along to the room where he had first kissed her, and went into it. For a moment, the wariness of fear was lost in the heat of emotion for her, and almost carelessly he opened the cupboard. The airline bag was there, zipped up. He pulled it out, and as he did he had the sensation as if he were touching her.

He turned and in that moment saw

the door moving shut. The opening was on the far side of him, against the wall. With a sudden swing he flung the bag into the corner between the frame and the edge of the door, then jumped on the bed and leapt down the other side. The door bumped on the bag and started to open again as the man outside let go the handle.

Allison came to the door, stood behind it for a moment, listening. There were soft footfalls, but he could not tell which way they went; he just knew they were drawing away and he opened the door and looked round the edge of the frame.

On his left the wreck of the centre roof blocked the way, and only streaks of daylight beamed through cracks in the broken wood and brick. To his right, the corridor was empty.

All the doors down the corridor stood open, just as he had passed them, and in one or more, somebody was hiding, waiting. The gun was sticky with sweat in his hand and his thumb pushed the safety catch.

It would not budge.

He drew back a pace into the room and looked at the mechanism. The catch was jammed solid, perhaps where it had been dropped.

Perhaps that was why Franz had thrown it away in the hall below. It was now good only for a bluff.

He picked up the bag again and peered round the edge of the door frame. Nothing moved in the corridor, but as he watched the stillness he heard the soft tread of feet going down the end stairs. There was no doubt about it, for he could recognise the squeaking of the treads.

He moved out and along the corridor, pausing at each doorway to listen before he went on. The squeaking of the stairs stopped and there was silence again but for the chuckling of the broken water pipe in the distance.

It seemed they had only one man up on the first floor.

Then, with staggering clarity, the answer to the whole of the strange affair came to him. For a moment he stopped still, staring at the end of the corridor, as if unable to believe it.

The water gurgled from the burst pipe, and far away the birds shrilled. He gripped the handle of the bag, and a slow, humourless grin spread across his face. He began to move slowly towards the stairs, then stopped and listened again.

No sound. The man below was waiting.

He turned back, moving quickly and without any noise, back to the girl's room. He went to the window where the bird had been trapped, and climbed out on to the sill. The old flower bed below was hairy with grass, but still soft. He dropped down into it. A swallow, startled by the movement, dashed shrilly away from the eaves in a long curve towards the trees. Nothing else seemed to notice.

Allison stood amidst the overgrown bushes and looked along the house front. He watched the shuttered windows of the big room, the only one where the shutters had been pulled and bolted. He put the bag down.

The grin spread on his face. They

wanted him inside the house, in the deliberate shadows amid the tottering ruins, but he was out now in the daylight.

They would have to come for him.

He moved quietly along the house front to the front door. It bulged now, its surrounds cracked and wrinkled where the second explosion had belched it out from the kitchen. He watched the wreckage through the opening and moved on to the broken wall of the west wing.

In his mind's eye he could see a grey figure padding quietly through the corridors in the remains of the house, looking for him; he could almost feel the seeker's growing alarm at finding him gone.

He must come out into the light now, the seeker.

Allison moved along the front of the ruins, and the sun burnt his bare flesh and the dull sting of his wounds faded before the fire of excitement.

He thought of the girl and remembered the thrill of touching her, of kissing her, and the odd sensation of fear that had come when Franz had returned silently up the stairs. He felt it again then, but it was like a thrill, adding, somehow to the excitement the girl gave him.

He came round the corner of the ruined wall and stared across the battlefield of wreckage to where the hall door had been. He was surprised to see that it still stood, and darkness gaped behind it where wreckage had blocked the hall.

In the still heat of the summer morning, the bird cries seemed to fade away as he watched the place.

Slowly he began to clamber over the rubble towards the hall door. He did not bother to look around him, but kept his eyes ahead, on the remains of the house. He knew they must come from there.

He went on, taking no cover, certain now there would be no shot fired. Whatever happened here had to look natural, had to look like an accident, misadventure, something that no later investigation could reveal as murder, for Jim had been here already and so the line was established and sooner or later, someone else must come along it, and there must be no bullets for him to find when he did come.

The heat seemed to whisper around him as he went on towards the old centre part of the house, some instinct drawing him as surely as he knew now that Jim's death had done.

Somewhere, dead ahead, a few yards off, were the hidden ones, the shadows, the relentless trackers who had followed them for so long.

But he knew what they were now; the puzzle was complete in his mind.

As he drew nearer the mass of shadows beneath the tumbled hall wall, he saw a movement. He stopped dead. There could be no mistaking the sudden action in the depths of the shadows beneath the fallen timber.

Suddenly, there was a shifting of wood, and a man, face blackened, and apparently blinded by the light, staggered out into the sun, his hands reaching out before him.

'Franz!' Allison said.

Franz seemed dazed, holding his hands to shield his eyes.

'Franz,' Allison said, between his teeth.

274

'Franz, I know you!'

Franz became quite still, his arms at his sides his fingers crooked. Allison went over the rubble to him, and as he got within two feet he swung a blow at Franz's head that rocked the man backwards. Allison trampled on and hit again. The fire in him made the pain in his fist a thing of fierce delight as he saw the powerful man driven back, hurt and stumbling.

Franz tripped and went down on all fours. He stayed there a moment looking up at his assailant. Allison wanted to drive his foot into the man's face, and only revulsion of the act stopped him. That hesitation lost him his chance against a man better versed in the warfare of the modern jungle.

Franz reached out suddenly and shoved a beam lengthways along the ground, taking Allison's left foot. The act was so swift and unexpected that Allison half turned and staggered to one side. In the moment that he was thrown off balance, Franz sprang up bringing the beam up with him. He raised it above his head and hurled it. The heavy balk struck Allison across his bare back and sent him sprawling headlong into the dust and bricks near the sentinel dining chair. As he went down, Franz leapt across the intervening space, picked up a brick and went to drive it down on Allison's head.

Allson twisted and as he did so, kicked upwards with his foot. The sole kicked Franz in the groin with the force of the man's own impetus, and with a grunt of pain he lost his aim and the brick crashed into the rubble by Allison's head.

Allison kicked himself clear with the swiftness of desperation and got to his knees as Franz came for him again. Even as he saw the man bearing down on him, Franz stopped dead, and a slow smile spread on his lowering face. He bent, quite slowly and picked up part of a broken beam. Allison remained as if hypnotised by the calculated slowness of the man's actions.

Then Allison moved. He sprang backwards from his crouching position, and as he went the beam smashed down into the dust beside him and he felt the vibration of it. He snatched up a brick and slung it almost from where it lay. It hit Franz's arm, and in the moment of pain while the man took another aim with the beam weapon, Allison went back still further, past the sentinel chair, then saw a piece of broken wood five feet long and grabbed it up as Franz bore down on him again, bringing down a terrible blow towards Allison's head. Allison put up his beam to defend himself. The shock of the smash burnt the tendons in his forearms, and the wood he held cracked and gave in the middle. But it had broken the force of the blow, which went aside. He went back again passing the chair. For a moment, Franz did not follow, then he tramped forward over the rubble, eyes blazing, his teeth showing in a grin of death. Allison recognised it as the broken wood fell from his numbed fingers. He stumbled backwards watching desperately, waiting for the moment when Franz would begin to bring down the final blow.

Franz struck. Allison twisted and the

beam seared down his left arm, tearing the skin, but crashing on into the rubble. Franz gave a grunt and raised the beam again. Allison's left foot was on a loose brick and as he went to back again, it rocked and slithered away beneath him. He fell backwards into the muck, and saw Franz towering above him, the beam raised over his head.

This was it. Allison could not move any more. Some last paralysing despair held him still, waiting for the blow to come.

Franz stood a massive figure against the sky, the master. The beam was back over his right shoulder, his great body muscles gathering to bring down the final blow.

And then suddenly, the muscles contracted. The grin on his face faded, and his eyes ceased to glare down at his victim. Instead they raised slowly, widening, in a terrible despair. The beam dropped down behind his back, raising a little cloud of dust, and as it did, Allison heard the distant tiny crack of a rifle shot.

Franz's hands dropped and pressed against his stomach. His mouth began to open and then he staggered forward, as if he were drunk. Allison went to one side on his hands and knees. The man tripped, began to half run over the rubble, then fell to his knees. His head toppled forward and he went slowly over the edge of the well in the attitude of a man making obeisance to Death. There seemed to be no sound until there came a distant brushing sound from the great depths.

Gasping, Allison got to his feet and stared back at the stable door. He saw Kate leaning back against the car boot, the slim little rook rifle standing against her. She looked as if with the shot, all life had left her body.

He stood for a while breathing the soft air as if it was something he had never known before. Then he went slowly back across the rubble. He watched her all the way. He saw her cover her face with her hands and stand there, sobbing, though he could hear nothing but the sounds of the birds.

As he went nearer to her a great emotion welled in him. He made no sound, but when he stopped before her she knew he was there. She dropped her hands and raised her tear-stained face, and there was a defiant line to her beautiful neck.

'I had to choose,' she said, and tears welled anew in her lovely eyes. She gave a little sob, then limped forward into his arms. 'Oh, Franz, Franz!' she moaned.

He held her tightly.

'No,' he said gently. 'Don't be sorry for Franz. It was he who tried to kill you. It was Franz in the mine down there, it was Franz locked us in the cellar. That's why he had to stay unseen. He had to keep up the play that some enemy had arrived.'

Slowly she lifted her head from his shoulder and looked into his eyes, the frown of shock and unbelief growing bright.

'How could it be?' she whispered. 'He loved me. He would hardly let me out of his sight.'

'But you didn't love him,' Allison said quietly.

Her eyes changed focus as if she looked through him to something else far off, and she shook her head very slightly.

'No. But there is a great emotion that comes with gratitude, and it is difficult to tell the difference between that and love sometimes. He was going to save me. That was such a big thing. No, no.' She shook her head again. 'I didn't love him, but I didn't know it until you came — ' He felt her shiver. 'And jealousy made him want to kill me — '

'Not that alone,' he said. 'The fact is that when he knew we had fallen as we did, he had to do something. You were the guardian of his secret, as he was of yours. When you heard the boat groaning, he got frightened. He *knew* that nobody else was in the place. He had rigged the stage, done the play-acting to try and frighten you to depend on him still, but most of all, when he nearly murdered both of us by starting a fall of wreckage on top of us he had to invent somebody beside himself. If he hadn't done, we would both have known long before. He hid that body because he was frightened to leave it there once it had been exposed, and by pretending he did not know who'd done it, strengthened the idea that somebody else was here. Also, it might have been useful to make you admit I was still alive . . . '

She seemed hardly to hear him.

'And he knew all his way into the darkness, into the mine, how to follow when we were lost — '

'He knew about this place from his father,' Allison said. 'This house had been kept empty for an owner who was abroad and never came back to it. But the owners never meant to come back. They used it to get their agents in — just as they got you in.'

'No.' Her voice was suddenly firm. 'No, you are wrong. I didn't come this way. I'm no part of an organisation. I came to see a friend, and they traced me, and they found me, and it was when I was invited to the Embassy that I was told why I had been brought there. They wanted me to give away — my own brother. That's why I shot. And that's why I ran.'

'Why run here?'

'Because once my brother mentioned it to me, as if it was something very important to him. And if, if I came to find him and could not, I should come here. And I did, in a panic, but instead of Willi, there was only Franz. But Franz seemed to know my trouble, he seemed to know about my brother, and he promised that he would get me away. I would have to wait, he said, and I did wait — but his friends never came — '

He held her tightly to him.

'The best thing,' he said, 'is to get right away from here. Another man like Jim must come soon. You can't be here then. It'll take time to get things fixed for you.'

'Can it be done?'

'It could be,' he said. 'I never heard of the murder in any Embassy. They keep these things hushed up, especially in cases like this. No, we must go and have time to think.'

'And you?' she said tenderly. 'Can you be fixed?'

He looked at her anxious eyes and then began to smile.

'I don't care any more,' he said. 'If we both have time to think I feel that anything's possible for us.'

He held her until it hurt and kissed her eyes and her nose and her cheeks and her lips. Then he swept her up into his arms and put her into the car seat.

'Come on,' he said, taking up his jacket. 'Let's go.'

'I must get something to wear,' she said as they backed out into the sun. 'I can't go like this.'

'Now I know you're a woman,' he said and drove slowly round to the front of the house. He stopped and got out and went back to where he had dropped the airline bag. He picked it up and turned, and there was the man standing on the green-patched drive watching him with his head cocked, a quizzical, almost amused look in his eyes. He looked up at the broken building, then mockingly back to Allison.

'I suppose it's as good a time as any

to leave,' the man said. 'Not much of it left, is there?'

'There was a marsh-gas explosion,' Allison said. 'Nearly blew us all to hell.'

'That's interesting,' the man said, bringing cigarettes from his pocket and glancing towards the car. 'Smoke?'

Allison took a cigarette.

'We are trying to trace some kind of subterranean explosion,' the man said. 'It's very odd. A few hours back a small under-water craft came to the surface ten miles out from the Bay.' He pointed over the trees. 'It seems to have been depth-charged, but of course, they don't let off depth charges these days.'

The man looked steadily at him.

'A sub?' said Allison, pretending surprise. 'Surely we don't blow up our own subs?'

'So innocent,' the man sighed, and savoured a long draw on his cigarette. 'It wasn't ours. What are you doing here?'

'I knew the place, years ago, and came to see it.'

Kate was keeping well down in the car

so that the stranger could not see how she was dressed.

'You were here when the blow-up came?' Again the man raked the building with his eyes.

'Yes. We got a bit damaged. Put us out for a bit. We're off to find a doctor. But why are you here if it's a sub you're after?'

'They take siesmograph plots back at the university other end of the bay. Seems the earthquake registers from a point about here between the lake and the sea-bed eight miles out.'

Allison looked back at the car.

'My wife has been shaken pretty badly,' he said. 'Do you mind if we leave you?'

A faint light of amusement gleamed in the man's eyes.

'Of course not,' he said. 'But just in case — a phone number perhaps?'

He took out a ballpoint and a small pad.

'Allison,' was the reply, and a telephone number was added.

The man smiled as he went back to the car, carrying the bag, Allison got in and

286

drove away through the quiet summer morning.

They slipped past the overhanging rock and the calm lake and the shadows of the trees flecked and fled across them.

'You gave him a phone number?' she said.

'Yes. He seemed to need it.'

'Then you are not going back?' she asked shrewdly.

'I'm starting out anew,' he said. 'And I certainly wouldn't go back to that number.'

'Why?' she asked sharply.

'I was once there because of an accident,' he said. 'It's the number of Muswell Hill Police Station.'

And the little trees danced as they brushed the sides of the car and the shadows raced and flickered over them, and the air was warm and exciting and everything was new. She snuggled deep in the seat and just sat there, staring ahead at nothing. He could almost feel the torment and the sadness in her and his heart grew big with a helpless kind of love for her.

And then they came out of the trees, and the sun was bright and very clear, and suddenly he knew the answer to the man called Franz. He had misconstrued the jealousy, which had been the jealousy of protection, not possession. The girl had misled him, created from Franz a lover who did not exist for her, but to cover up his real identity. This had been the man the Embassy thought had begun to doublecross them, just as he had turned on Kate and tried to kill her when he thought he could trust her no more. Yet even when he was dead, she had kept the pretence that they had loved each other as strangers, to defend his memory.

But now Franz was dead and his crimes dead with him. Yet she must suffer for a loyalty that stayed, despite everything he had done to her, after her brother was dead.

A LANCE FOR THE DEVIL
Robert Charles

The funeral service of Pope Paul VI was to be held in the great plaza before St. Peter's Cathedral in Rome, and was to be the scene of the most monstrous mass assassination of political leaders the world had ever known. Only Counter-Terror could prevent it.

IN THAT RICH EARTH
Alan Sewart

How long does it take for a human body to decay until only the bones remain? When Detective Sergeant Harry Chamberlane received news of a body, he raised exactly that question. But whose was the body? Who was to blame for the death and in what circumstances?

MURDER AS USUAL
Hugh Pentecost
A psychotic girl shot and killed Mac Crenshaw, who had come to the New England town with the advance party for Senator Farraday. Private detective David Cotter agreed that the girl was probably just a pawn in a complex game — but who had sent her on the assignment?

THE MARGIN
Ian Stuart
It is rumoured that Walkers Brewery has been selling arms to the South African army, and Graham Lorimer is asked to investigate. He meets the beautiful Shelley van Rynveld, who is dedicated to ending apartheid. When a Walkers employee is killed in a hit-and-run accident, his wife tells Graham that he's been seeing Shelly van Rynveld . . .

TOO LATE FOR THE FUNERAL
Roger Ormerod

Carol Turner, seventeen, and a mystery, is very close to a murder, and she has in her possession a weapon that could prove a number of things. But it is Elsa Mallin who suffers most before the truth of Carol Turner releases her.

NIGHT OF THE FAIR
Jay Baker

The gun was the last of the things for which Harry Judd had fought and now it was in the hands of his worst enemy, aimed at the boy he had tried to help. This was the night in which the past had to be faced again and finally understood.

PAY-OFF IN SWITZERLAND
Bill Knox

'Hot' British currency was being smuggled to Switzerland to be laundered, hidden in a safari-style convoy heading across Europe. Jonathan Gaunt, external auditor for the Queen's and Lord Treasurer's Remembrancer, went along with the safari, posing as a tourist, to get any lead he could. But sudden death trailed the convoy every kilometer to Lake Geneva.

SALVAGE JOB
Bill Knox

A storm has left the oil tanker S. S. *Craig Michael* stranded and almost blocking the only channel to the bay at Cabo Esco. Sent to investigate, marine insurance inspector Laird discovers that the Portuguese bay is hiding a powder keg of international proportions.

BOMB SCARE — FLIGHT 147
Peter Chambers

Smog delayed Flight 147, and so prevented a bomb exploding in mid-air. Walter Keane found that during the crisis he had been robbed of his jewel bag, and Mark Preston was hired to locate it without involving the police. When a murder was committed, Preston knew the stake had grown.

STAMBOUL INTRIGUE
Robert Charles

Greece and Turkey were on the brink of war, and the conflict could spell the beginning of the end for the Western defence pact of N.A.T.O. When the rumour of a plot to speed this possibility reached Counter-espionage in Whitehall, Simon Larren and Adrian Cleyton were despatched to Turkey . . .

CRACK IN THE SIDEWALK
Basil Copper

After brilliant scientist Professor Hopcroft is knocked down and killed by a car, L.A. private investigator Mike Faraday discovers that his death was murder and that differing groups are engaged in a power struggle for The Zetland Method. As Mike tries to discover what The Zetland Method is, corpses and hair-breadth escapes come thick and fast . . .

DEATH OF A MARINE
Charles Leader

When Mike M'Call found the mutilated corpse of a marine in an alleyway in Singapore, a thousand-strong marine battalion was hell-bent on revenge for their murdered comrade — and the next target for the tong gang of paid killers appeared to be M'Call himself . . .

ANYONE CAN MURDER
Freda Bream

Hubert Carson, the editorial Manager of the Herald Newspaper in Auckland, is found dead in his office. Carson's fellow employees knew that the unpopular chief reporter, Clive Yarwood, wanted Carson's job — but did he want it badly enough to kill for it?

CART BEFORE THE HEARSE
Roger Ormerod

Sometimes a case comes up backwards. When Ernest Connelly said 'I have killed . . . ', he did not name the victim. So Dave Mallin and George Coe find themselves attempting to discover a body to fit the crime.

SALESMAN OF DEATH
Charles Leader

For Mike M'Call, selling guns in Detroit proves a dangerous business — from the moment of his arrival in the middle of a racial riot, to the final clash of arms between two rival groups of militant extremists.

THE FOURTH SHADOW
Robert Charles

Simon Larren merely had to ensure that the visiting President of Maraquilla remained alive during a goodwill tour of the British Crown Colony of San Quito. But there were complications. Finally, there was a Communist-inspired bid for illegal independence from British rule, backed by the evil of voodoo.

SCAVENGERS AT WAR
Charles Leader

Colonel Piet Van Velsen needed an experienced officer for his mercenary commando, and Mike M'Call became a reluctant soldier. The Latin American Republic was torn apart by revolutionary guerrilla groups — but why were the ruthless Congo veterans unleashed on a province where no guerrilla threat existed?

MENACES, MENACES
Michael Underwood

Herbert Sipson, professional black-mailer, was charged with demanding money from a bingo company. Then, a demand from the Swallow Sugar Corporation also bore all the hallmarks of a Sipson scheme. But it arrived on the opening day of Herbert's Old Bailey trial — so how could he have been responsible?

MURDER WITH MALICE
Nicholas Blake

At the Wonderland holiday camp, someone calling himself The Mad Hatter is carrying out strange practical jokes that are turning increasingly malicious. Private Investigator Nigel Strangeways follows the Mad Hatter's trail and finally manages to make sense of the mayhem.

THE LONG NIGHT
Hartley Howard

Glenn Bowman is awakened by the 'phone ringing in the early hours of the morning and a woman he does not know invites him over to her apartment. When she tells him she wishes she was dead, he decides he ought to go and talk to her. It is a decision he is to bitterly regret when he finds himself involved in a case of murder . . .

THE LONELY PLACE
Basil Copper

The laconic L.A. private investigator Mike Faraday is hired to discover who is behind the death-threats to millionaire ex-silent movie star Francis Bolivar. Faraday finds a strange state of affairs at Bolivar's Gothic mansion, leading to a horrifying mass slaughter when a chauffeur goes berserk.